# Readers love A

## A Taste of Love

"…an emotional story that will have you in tears one minute, smiling and laughing the next."
—Love Romances & More

## A Shared Range

"…another enjoyable read filled with two well rounded and likable guys."
—Literary Nymphs

## An Unexpected Vintage

"There's nothing like a story that reminds you to get out and enjoy life!"
—Fallen Angel Reviews

## Love Means… Freedom

"Mr. Grey has, once again, brought to life compelling characters with whom readers can identify and about whom we can care deeply. This is one of those books best read snuggled up in a cozy, favorite chair while the wind howls outside."
—Whipped Cream Erotic Romance Reviews

## Accompanied by a Waltz

"A story about first love, loss, and the rediscovery of love all wrapped up in its pages."
—Fallen Angel Reviews

http://www.dreamspinnerpress.com

# DUTCH *Treat*

## ANDREW GREY

*Dreamspinner Press*

Published by
Dreamspinner Press
4760 Preston Road
Suite 244-149
Frisco, TX 75034
http://www.dreamspinnerpress.com/

Dutch Treat
Copyright © 2011 by Andrew Grey

Cover Art by Anne Cain    annecain.art@gmail.com
Cover Design by Mara McKennen

ISBN: 978-1-61372-057-8

Printed in the United States of America
First Edition
July 2011

eBook edition available
eBook ISBN: 978-1-61372-058-5

To Dominic, who supported me and loved me when I spent five months working in The Netherlands. We rarely saw each other during that time, but I knew he was always there for me.

# CHAPTER

One

THE sound of the ringing phone startled Michael out of his usual early-morning haze as he drove to work. He almost ignored it, but figured a call this early might be important so Michael pulled his old car off to the side of the road. "Hello."

"Morning, Mikey!"

"Devon." Michael couldn't help smiling. "How can you be so chipper at this God-awful hour of the morning?" Devon always seemed to have buckets of energy, day or night, and especially in bed.

"Are you on your way to work?" Devon asked, ignoring Michael's question.

"I'm in the car and should be there in ten minutes or so. Why?"

"No reason. I just wanted to catch you before you got there because I didn't want to disturb you at your office." Devon paused for a second, probably expecting Michael to say something, but he hadn't had his first cup of coffee yet and was only functioning on autopilot. "Are we still going out tonight? I've been looking forward to it all week. I even got a new shirt so I'll look good when we go out. I was thinking we could go to Boyztown tonight. They have the greatest music, and I can dance." Now, that was always a sight. Michael could never take his eyes off his lover when he danced. The only problem was that neither could anyone else.

"Yes, we're still on. I told you I'd take you out for your birthday, and I meant it." Something kicked in and Michael felt alert. "I'll pick you up at your place, and we can go to dinner first. Have a good day at work, and I'll see you tonight."

"Okay, you too," Devon replied excitedly before disconnecting. Michael's smile lasted all the way through the rest of his drive and until he was settled in his office, getting ready for his first meeting of the day. Thankfully, it was a Friday, and he only had to get through today and he would have two whole days of peace, fun, and Devon.

He and Devon had been seeing each other for the past six months, and it had been good, really good. Devon really didn't seem to mind that Michael was older. They were good together, and Devon had recently began using the L word quite a bit, which made Michael's heart jump every time.

"Are you going to stare at that screen all day or get some work done?" Kyle said from his door with a huge grin. Like Michael, Kyle was also an information systems project manager for Shoe Box, a worldwide retailer of athletic shoes, and they shared the same boss. But their similarities ended there. Where Michael was driven as far as his projects were concerned, Kyle had a laid-back attitude that Michael couldn't understand. Somehow, Kyle's projects seemed to come together out of thin air, while Michael worked very hard to make sure everything was the way it should be. It was infuriating, but Kyle was one of those guys no one could be mad at, and that included Michael.

"Sorry," Michael answered, "I haven't had my coffee yet."

"I think you'll want to get that coffee now. Curtis called a management meeting for eight thirty, and you know how he is," Kyle said after making sure the hallway was empty. Michael knew exactly how he was, even after having worked for the man only a few months. Curtis's changing moods were well-ingrained upon everyone who worked for him. Michael had often thought the man needed a good dose of mood stabilizers, but couldn't say that to anyone.

"Thanks for the warning." Michael opened his e-mail and saw the messages from Curtis sitting in his inbox like terrorist pipe bombs just waiting to ruin a perfectly good Friday. Ignoring them for now, Michael got up and accompanied Kyle down to the cafeteria, returning a few minutes later, coffee in hand, to go through his e-mails and prepare for his day and the infamous meeting.

At the appointed time, Michael got up from his desk and hurried to the conference room, finding the other managers already there and Curtis sitting at the head of the table, looking toward the door. Michael glanced at the clock just to make sure he wasn't late before closing the door and taking one of the empty chairs. Curtis had a real thing about being on time for meetings and appointments, even though the one person on the team most likely to be late for anything was Curtis himself. Every week, Curtis had a set time to meet with each of his managers, and more likely than not, Michael would be kept waiting for his appointment. But heaven forbid the world would end if he were a minute late for anything Curtis scheduled.

"We've been tasked with taking on an extra project because of the shuffles with the logistics team. They lost one of their project managers, and since our team still has two," Curtis said, as he turned to Kyle and Michael with one of his self-righteous "I fought for you, so you owe me" looks on his face. "I'll be reassigning the projects this morning, and things will need to change. Right now the workload isn't balanced, and this additional project is going to make things even more complicated. Brian, I'm going to need you to take on one of the projects. It'll be one of the simpler ones that fits with your team. Kyle and Michael, I haven't figured out how I'm going to divide things up yet, but I'll talk to both of you later this morning."

Michael felt his stomach lurch, but he was careful to keep any reaction off his face. He currently had three projects, and all three of them were well under control, fully planned, and carefully timelined. He'd spent months doing all the requirements-gathering, documentation, planning, and team building, working nights and even weekends to make sure they were right, and now who the hell knew what Curtis was going to come up with. After Curtis's little announcement, the man launched into stories that ate up almost the next half hour. Michael kept looking at the clock, wondering when he could get back to his desk. There was plenty to get done regardless of Curtis's project shakeup, and he had calls that needed to be made. Zoning out, Michael tried to organize everything in his head so that when he could get out of here, he could get right to work.

"So I woke up in the middle of the night, wet, and when I lifted the covers, my crotch was green. The bag of peas had leaked all over everything. Never refreeze the bag of peas. Once they thaw, throw them out." Everyone laughed, and Michael did as well because it was expected, even if he'd already heard the story of Curtis's vasectomy and the infamous bag of peas at least twice. Kyle had confessed after the last telling that he'd heard it at least six times. The only comforting thought about that story was that the world would be spared from any more "little Curtises"—there was a God after all.

Finally, the waste of time Curtis called a meeting was over, and Michael hurried back to his desk. Checking his e-mail once again, he found it blessedly empty and began making calls, ticking other tasks off his list as he verified that all critical tasks were on plan. The last call he made was to the software rep, Marty, to make sure they would deliver the customized store register code as promised. Their timeline for delivery was already tight and any slippage would delay the entire project. Michael did not want to have to explain that to Curtis, or for that matter to Mark, the vice president of the technology development. After being assured that everything was on track and that no problems had been found, they talked for a few minutes about Marty's new baby before disconnecting. Michael had known Marty for years and had worked hard under his previous director to build a good relationship.

Checking his list again, he set up meetings for the following week before starting to work on the next steps in his project documentation. Fridays were usually good days with limited meetings, which allowed him to get caught up, and if he were lucky, slightly ahead on the next week's work. "Michael." He looked up and saw Kyle peering into his office. "Curtis asked me to send you to his office."

Kyle definitely looked a little worse for wear, and Michael wondered just what had happened, but Kyle walked away without saying anything more. Michael picked up his day planner, and after locking his PC, walked down the hallway toward the front corner offices where the directors and vice presidents had their offices. Curtis's door was open, but he wasn't at his desk. Taking a seat in one of the chairs, Michael opened his planner, updating his to-do list with tasks he needed to do next week, until Curtis walked in and shut the door. Glancing at his watch, Michael realized he'd been waiting for almost fifteen minutes.

"As I said in the meeting this morning, we need to reassign some of the projects, but something else has come up since then." Curtis sat down in his leather office chair, fishing through the piles of crap on his desk. "The Shoe Finder project for Europe is in trouble. Europe doesn't have the resources to work with Kyle to complete the project. They have people to do the work, but not manage it from their end. They asked if we could send the project manager over there to work with their people until the project is completed at the end of October."

"So Kyle will be going to Europe for, what, five months?" Michael asked, trying to figure out which of Kyle's projects he could take over to help out. "What can I do to help?"

"That's the issue. Kyle isn't willing to be away from his family for that period of time, and Mark wanted me to ask if you'd take over the project. I want to stress that this is Kyle's project, and you don't have to do this." The last sentiments were added in a rush that rendered them completely meaningless. *In other words,* Michael read into it silently, *you don't have to do this, but Mark will remember that you weren't a team player and weren't willing to do what the company needed.* Since Kyle had a wife and kids, those things didn't seem to apply to him. Michael was speechless. He hadn't seen this coming at all, and now everything had been turned on its end. Curtis continued talking without waiting for Michael's response. "We'll move the Canada and Asia projects to Kyle, and transition the Europe project to you. You'll keep the automated-scheduling project since that's already being implemented."

"When do you need an answer?" Michael asked, bringing Curtis to a screeching halt, and Michael realized Curtis hadn't made any plans for what would happen if Michael said no. Curtis had simply assumed Michael would do it, and he probably would have for Dennis, his previous supervisor and one of the best people Michael had ever worked with.

"We need an answer as soon as possible, but you know if you pull this off, this could be a career-making move for you," Curtis said as he leaned forward, the part about the promotion that he knew Michael had been hoping for going unvocalized, but definitely implied.

Michael's throat felt dry. "Let me think about it."

"You did the US version of this project, so this shouldn't really be all that hard," Curtis told him, leaning back in his chair, and Michael could almost see him pull his salesman's hat out of the drawer. "And you'll get to spend some time in Europe. Have you ever been?" Curtis inquired, his voice taking on an edge of excitement.

"No, I haven't," Michael answered, feeling a twinge of excitement himself. "I need some time to think about this," he said, checking his watch, "and I have a meeting in a few minutes."

"Get back to me this afternoon, and we can hammer out any details." Curtis turned his attention to his computer, and Michael realized he'd been dismissed. Opening the office door, Michael stepped out and saw Mark walking down the hallway toward him.

"Did Curtis talk to you?" Mark asked as he approached. "You'd be doing us all a big favor if you'd do this," Mark told him, tilting his head back toward his office, and Michael followed him, taking a seat inside the plush, well-decorated office. "We shouldn't have to ask you to do this. This is Kyle's project, and I'm none too happy that he isn't willing to go. I also understand that we're asking a lot of you to go, but you've always stepped up for us in the past. Even when your plate was full, you never complained when anyone needed anything. You just somehow got a bigger plate, and I'm afraid we need that now." Mark sat in his chair, hands on his desk, full attention on Michael. "If you do this, we'll get you an apartment outside Amsterdam so you won't be living in a hotel the entire time, although you probably will for a few weeks until we can make the arrangements, and we'll fly you back to the States every four or five weeks. The European division will provide you with one of their leased cars, and of course you'll be on expenses the entire time."

"This is a lot to take in," Michael said.

"Yes, but you're single, and things like this are easier for you than some of the other guys," Mark explained.

"That doesn't mean I don't have a life," Michael countered, and he saw the surprise in Mark's expression. "Curtis said the same thing you did, not in so many words, and I take exception with that argument. I may not be married or have children, but I have a life and people I love, who, if I accept this, I'll be leaving behind for weeks at a time."

"I know," Mark explained, backpedaling a little. "I didn't mean to belittle the effect on anyone's life. This assignment will require some sacrifice on your part, but I wanted you to know that we'll take care of you and we'll owe you one."

"Okay," Michael said steadily, "I'll think about it and let you know this afternoon."

"I can't ask for any more than that," Mark told him as he nodded his head, and Michael got up from the chair, leaving the office, passing Curtis on the way. He smiled at him, but neither of them stopped to talk, and Michael went straight back to his office, shutting the door. Picking up the phone, he dialed the number for the call he was very nearly late for.

Half an hour later, he hung up, but left his door closed. He needed to think, and a steady stream of people asking him questions was not going to help him do that. Just when he'd gotten both his work and home life in order, something had to come and throw everything all out of whack. The thought of the chance to spend some time in Europe was enticing. He'd never been out of the country before, except to across the borders to Canada and Mexico, so at least he had a passport. Six months ago, he'd have jumped at this chance, but six months ago he hadn't met Devon and started a relationship. At least he hadn't bought a house yet, although he'd been looking for a few months. Picking up the phone, he dialed the one person he knew he could rely on for sound advice.

"Dennis, it's Michael," he said when his former boss answered the phone.

"Hey, how's it going? You miss me yet?" Dennis asked with a smile in his voice.

"Every day," Michael answered. "Are you and Carol getting settled?"

"She found a house she loves and then said she was pregnant again, so I've got plenty to keep me busy getting everything ready for the baby." Dennis laughed and Michael joined in. He knew getting the new house ready for another child meant writing the checks for anything Carol decided she wanted to have done. Dennis was not a hands-on kind of guy. "How are things there?"

"Exactly as you expected."

"I'm sorry about that. I was hoping I was wrong, and let me guess, they're now asking you to pick up the slack."

"They want me to go to Europe for five months or so to run the Shoe Finder project for them."

"Why isn't Kyle going? It's his project. After you did the US, he begged me to give him Europe, said he wanted to try something new." Michael could hear the frustration in Dennis's voice. "I guess I shouldn't be too surprised. Have you decided what you want to do?"

"I really don't want to go. Things are good here right now." Michael knew Dennis understood what he meant. Dennis was the coolest boss he'd ever had. Dennis had understood when he and Devon had started dating. He'd even encouraged him to get out of the office and find someone. It had been Dennis who had plucked Michael out of near obscurity from the small office in Dayton, promoting, encouraging, and helping him build the skills to be a good project manager. They'd worked well together for the past three years. Dennis deserved his promotion; there was no doubt about that. Michael just wished he'd been promoted within the same facility instead of half the country away.

"I know they are, but this could be a once-in-a-career opportunity. A lot of people are going to be looking at this project, and not just in the US, but in Europe as well, and right now that's where the growth is." Dennis started to chuckle. "Think about it, you'll be six time zones and three thousand miles away from Curtis."

Michael could barely hold back his laugh. "They want an answer this afternoon."

"No one can make your decision for you, but decide what you want and stick to it. If you decide to do this, they owe you—make sure they know and understand that. You know I won't let them forget it, either. Mark and I are now colleagues, so I report to the same people he does."

"Thanks."

"I wish I could talk more, but I have an appointment. Let me know what you decide." Dennis hung up, and Michael stood, walking over and opening his door before going back to work. At lunchtime, he ate alone. Usually Michael ate with some of the guys or other managers, but today he wasn't up for it. He had too much to think about. What bothered him most was that he knew he was going to do it. He knew he'd put his life on hold and do this project because they'd asked, but he absolutely didn't want to go. It wasn't in his psyche to turn them down. Michael had always done what the company needed and asked of him, and it really wasn't in him to say no. He knew it, and he thought Curtis and Mark knew it too.

His cell phone vibrated in his pocket, and Michael fished it out. Devon—that was another complication. They'd been going out for six months, and Michael was developing feelings for the man with deep blue eyes and blond curls that always flopped in his face. He certainly didn't want to spend almost the entire summer away from him. Michael had definitely been looking forward to spending time with Devon at one of the local lakes, swimming and lying in the sun next to him, pretending to read while he secretly watched every move and breath Devon made.

"Hi, Devon," Michael said with more energy than he was feeling.

"Is everything okay? I thought I'd call and see how your day was going." Devon sounded so happy and totally sweet.

"Could be better," Michael answered without further explanation.

"Are we still on for tonight?" Some of the excitement slipped from his voice. "We really don't have to if you're not up to it, I guess."

"No. I promised to take you dancing, and I meant it. I'll pick you up at your place at six, and we'll go to dinner, dancing for a while, and then back to my apartment. And I don't plan on letting you leave the rest of the weekend. So please pack a bag. I'll even make pancakes tomorrow morning."

"That's a deal," Devon nearly squealed into the phone. "I get out of work at five, so I'll definitely be home at six." Devon hung up, and Michael shoved his phone back into his pocket before leaving to go to Curtis's office. He figured he might as well get this over with.

MICHAEL pulled in front of Devon's apartment building a few minutes before six. The car had barely stopped when he saw Devon hurrying down the steps carrying a small suitcase, and rushing to the car. The man looked as sweet as Michael had ever seen anyone, curls bouncing with each step, tight black T-shirt and leather pants, in other words, sex on wheels. Michael got out of the car to open the trunk and practically got tackled instead. "I missed you too," Michael said as Devon squeezed him before angling for a kiss, which he got, standing in the parking lot or not. Michael had learned very early that Devon was out and proud. "Let's put your bag in the trunk, and we'll go to dinner."

"Can we get Chinese? I'm hungry for sweet and sour," Devon asked as he put his suitcase in the trunk, closing the lid.

"Sure. We can go anywhere you want."

Devon stopped and looked at him. "Okay. What's wrong that you don't want to tell me?"

"Who said anything was wrong?" Michael tried to look surprised but gave it up. He should have known Devon would see right through him.

"You hate Chinese. So I know the only time you ever agree to go there is when you're trying to make something up to me. You may as well spill it because you know I'll just dig and dig until you tell me." Devon was like a dog with a bone when it came to secrets or any kind of news.

"I was going to wait until tomorrow, but I'll tell you over dinner if you promise not to let it ruin our weekend." Michael climbed into the driver's seat and started the engine, waiting for Devon to buckle up. It only took five minutes before they arrived at Devon's favorite Chinese place. Devon was right, Michael really didn't like Chinese food, but Devon did and this was for him. The hostess sat them at an out-of-the-way table, and after bringing a pot of tea, left them alone.

"So what's this news?"

"I have a new project and part of it is that I need to go to Europe."

"Can I go too? I have vacation time built up." The hopeful look on Devon's face twisted Michael's stomach.

"Devon, I have to do a project for the European division. I'll be away in Europe for five or six months." Michael watched as Devon's face fell, his smile changing to confusion and then a scowl. "I'll be back about once a month for a week, but the rest of the time I'll need to be working out of the Europe office."

"Oh," Devon said as he set his tea back on the table, staring at Michael like it was Christmas morning and Michael had just broken the toy he'd waited all year for. "So you're leaving me."

"No, I hope not." Michael reached across the table to touch Devon's hand. "I have to do this project. I was sort of thinking that this summer you could come over to visit me. I could take vacation time, and we could see things." He had no idea what they would see, but he could figure it out.

"Yeah, I could, but you'll still be gone for most of the summer, and I'll hardly ever see you." Devon was clearly disappointed, and part of Michael was happy that Devon was going to miss him, but he hated disappointing him. "I know you'll be back, but only a few times." Devon played with his now-empty teacup. "I know you didn't have a choice and that this wasn't your idea, but...." Devon looked down at the table, twisting the cup in his fingers nervously.

"Devon, I'd take you with me if I could. But you have to work, and much of the time that I'm there, I'll be working too. This isn't by my own choice, but I have to go."

The server interrupted them to take their orders. She had to ask Devon three times what he wanted because he just didn't seem to be listening, and eventually Michael ordered for him and she left. Reaching across the table, Michael untwisted Devon's hands from the cup, touching his fingers. "You know I would if I could."

"I know," Devon said softly. "When do you have to leave?"

"Not until after Memorial Day. I'll be gone most of June, but I'll be back for Fourth of July weekend, and I thought that you could come for a visit if you wanted, probably the last weekend in July." Michael was trying, but Devon just wasn't giving him much to work with.

Finally Devon raised his eyes. "Could we visit Paris?"

Michael smiled, some of the worry in his stomach edging away. "We can go wherever you want." Michael squeezed Devon's fingers lightly. "I'll have an apartment and a car, so we'll be able to go all over and see everything," Michael clarified, not really knowing what he was talking about, but some of the light came back into Devon's eyes, and that was always good. "I know this is a lot to take in, but do you think we can put this aside at least for the weekend and just enjoy ourselves?"

"Yes, I'll try," Devon answered just before the server brought their plates, and Devon began to eat. The smaller man usually packed away the food, and tonight was no exception. Michael ate his kung pao chicken as Devon wolfed down his sweet and sour pork, two eggrolls, and the plate of fortune cookies the server brought when they had cleaned their plates.

"My news doesn't seem to have affected your appetite," Michael commented with a smile, and Devon peered back at him, curls flopping partially into his eyes. Damn, the man looked adorably beautiful, and Michael wanted to ask if they could skip the dancing and just go right back to his place, but he knew Devon was looking forward to going out, and he wouldn't disappoint him, not twice in the same evening.

"You're right, Michael. We have this weekend and the next few weeks, and I can either mope because you're going away or I can make the most of it." Devon's eyes danced with a mixture of excitement and smoldering passion that nearly had Michael moaning out loud right there in the restaurant. "So let's pay the check and go downtown." Devon stood up, straightening his shirt. "I'm ready to make you forget all about everything but me." Good God, if Devon didn't give him a look that dripped pure sex, and the temptation to carry him home like a caveman asserted itself again.

Instead, Michael stood up as well, picking up the check and taking it to the cashier with Devon right behind him, so close he could hear his clothes rustle and smell the scent of his cologne—not overpowering, simply Devon. After Michael paid the bill, they walked out to the car, and Michael waited for Devon to settle in his seat before leaning over to kiss him. Then he started the car and drove out of town to the freeway.

It took half an hour, and an additional fifteen minutes to find a parking space, but then he and Devon walked down the bustling sidewalk to the club that Devon had chosen. Michael hadn't been to clubs much, they weren't really his style, but Devon loved them and Michael loved being with Devon, so they went occasionally. At the door, Michael could hear the loud techno dance music pouring out of the club. He paid their admission and followed Devon into the club, where men stood around drinking, watching each other, and a few of them were actually dancing. "Let's get something to drink," Michael said, leading Devon to the bar, where Michael found his companion created quite a stir, with most of the other guys turning to look at Devon. He paid no attention, much to Michael's relief, and after getting their drinks, Michael followed Devon to an empty table. Sitting down, Michael watched people for a while as they sipped their drinks, Devon's hand in his.

"I'm gonna dance," Devon announced as he stood up and downed the last of his Manhattan. "Come with me."

"You know I look like an idiot whenever I dance."

Devon laughed out loud. "I know, but I still want to dance with you." There was no way Michael could say no to that, so he followed Devon onto the dance floor, swaying a little to the music while Devon moved and gyrated around him. The man was sexy as hell with the way his entire body seemed to flow, and those hips, flexing and gyrating in his direction.

A tall, dark-skinned man in a shiny white shirt moved between them, matching Devon's movements, and Michael simply stood and watched for a few seconds until the other man put his hands on Devon's hips, pulling the two of them together. Devon stepped away, moving closer to Michael, who scowled at the other man, and he moved away, dancing with the next guy on the floor. Devon pulled him closer and continued dancing, his lithe body slinking and twirling around the dance floor.

"Mikey," Devon said over the music, still dancing, "can we go home now?" Michael smiled and began doing a dance of his very own that ended when he and Devon walked through the door to his apartment and fell together on his bed, beginning a very different kind of dance.

# CHAPTER
## *Two*

MICHAEL'S alarm went off, and he hurried out of bed, jumping into the shower before dressing in his most comfortable clothes. He'd asked Devon to stay last night, but Devon had backed away, not that Michael could really blame him. The past two weeks had been special. They'd spent a lot of time together, but as the days passed, Michael had felt Devon beginning to pull away, and he didn't know what to do about it. The buzzer rang and Michael answered it, opening the door as he got his suitcases. "Mikey," Devon called from the door before walking in, "are you ready to go?"

"Yes. I'm in the living room," Michael called as he picked up his carry-on bag before setting it down again, checking it one last time to make sure he had everything.

"Mikey, how many times have you checked that?"

"At least eight," Michael answered, looking up to see Devon staring at him, and he knew—just by the way Devon's eyes held that touch of sorrow, nervousness, and shame—he'd go to Europe and Devon would stay here. There would be no Devon coming to visit him, and he wouldn't be coming back to the States to spend his weeks in town with his boyfriend.

"Michael, I'm sorry," Devon said, swallowing. "I thought...."

"I know," Michael responded without letting Devon finish, letting him off the hook, because there was no need to drag this out for either of them. While Devon hadn't said anything, Michael had known he was trying to be understanding. But Devon wasn't happy about him leaving, and there was nothing Michael could do about it. "It's okay." *What else could he say?*

"I'm sorry, Mikey. I just can't sit around all summer and wait for you to come back every few weeks. I like you, a lot, but I'm not really sure where we were going anyway."

"I understand," Michael answered, "I really do." He and Devon had always been very compatible in bed, but even Michael had to admit that while he liked Devon, he probably wasn't the love of his life. "I just wish you'd have said something a little sooner rather than the day I'm leaving."

"I was going to, but then you'd call or suggest something fun, and I didn't have the heart." Devon sat on the sofa looking up at him, blond curls falling in his eyes. "I know I'm probably being a jerk for doing it this way, but the last two weeks have been fun. Hell, the last six months have been incredible, but I don't think we're in this for the long haul, ya know?" Michael wanted to say something, but Devon stood up, touching his lips with a finger. "We need to get your bags in my car so you don't miss your flight."

Michael nodded blankly and picked up a suitcase and his carry-on while Devon grabbed the other bag. He didn't know what to say and found himself lapsing into silence. He could hardly believe that Devon was breaking up with him today of all days. Not that any day was a particularly great day to break up with someone. But Michael had come to care for Devon a great deal, and he'd been happy—Devon had made him happy. Stowing the bags in the trunk, Michael checked out his apartment one more time before locking up and getting in the car.

The ride to the airport was an exercise in avoiding all conversation. Michael didn't know what to say, and obviously Devon didn't either. The sound of the road under the tires was the only sound that filled the car nearly the entire trip.

"Mikey, I didn't want to hurt you. I know I did, but I really didn't want that." Devon pulled off the freeway and onto the airport approaches. "I care for you, I really do, and I probably always will." Devon pulled up to the terminal. "You were very good to me and treated me wonderfully," Devon told him, and Michael saw a tear roll down

Devon's face. "No one ever treated me the way you did, and I'll always remember and be grateful to you for that."

"I don't know quite what to say." Michael felt a little lost.

"Just say good-bye. I hope everything works out for you. I'd love it if you'd call me when you come back to town."

"You want to be friends?"

"We were friends before we became lovers. You need and deserve more than I can give you." Devon popped the trunk and opened his door. Michael got out as well, getting his bags from the trunk before closing the lid. "Good-bye, Mikey. Have a good trip." He felt Devon's lips brush over his and, opening his eyes, saw the trail of tears on his face.

"Good-bye, Devon," he said as he watched Devon step away and get back into his car. Michael didn't move until Devon's car disappeared from sight. Slinging his carry-on over his shoulder, he picked up his suitcases and walked into the airport. There was nothing else he could do standing out in front of the terminal. Hoping Devon would come back and tell him this was all a joke probably wasn't a viable option, so he got in line and waited his turn. The woman behind the counter checked his passport and flight information before checking his bags to Amsterdam and handing him his boarding passes.

Sort of on autopilot, Michael walked in the direction the ticket agent indicated, making his way through security, turning hopefully to look one last time, just in case. After practically undressing so he could get through the checkpoint, Michael put his shoes and belt back on before gathering the rest of his things and heading to his gate for his quick flight from Harrisburg, Pennsylvania, to Dulles, which boarded and left on time, giving Michael plenty of time to relax before his transatlantic flight. He grabbed a bite to eat, hardly tasting his food, and wandered a little around the terminal until his flight was called. Waiting in line again, he handed his boarding pass to the attendant and walked down the Jetway. Around him, people talked excitedly, but Michael felt alone and apprehensive. He'd never been in a foreign country before, not across an ocean, and his nerves were starting to get the better of him. Finding his seat, he placed his bag in the overhead bin.

"Would you be so kind?" a small voice said from behind him, and Michael turned to see a diminutive woman who had to be approaching eighty struggling with her bag.

"Of course," Michael said with a smile, taking the bag from her and easily placing it in the bin before letting her take her seat. Checking his assignment again, he took the seat next to hers, getting comfortable before fishing in the pocket in front of him for the magazine.

"Have you flown before?"

"Yes, ma'am," he answered. "I'm Michael, by the way."

"Ruth Ann, most everybody calls me Ruthie. I'm going to Amsterdam to visit my son and his wife," she added proudly. "Actually, I'm going to see my grandson." She leaned closer. "If I can lose them, I plan to try some of the pot in one of those coffeehouses." For a second, Michael wasn't sure she was serious. "My husband and I were quite the couple in the sixties. I haven't had any good reefer in years. Not since I had children."

Michael thought he was going to choke for a second and then began to laugh. "Well, good for you." He leaned close to her and said, "I tried it once in college—made me act really silly. My roommate and his friends videotaped me kissing one of our dorm windows. To this day, I don't know why I was trying to do that, but they have video proof." Michael laughed and Ruthie joined him. "So it's not likely you'll see me there. But I hope you have a great time." Michael lapsed into silence, thumbing through the magazine. People continued boarding, occasionally bumping his arm, and he kept leaning away from the aisle.

"I remember when flying was really something special," Ruthie said from the next seat, and Michael set the magazine aside. He hadn't really been reading it, anyway. "The first time I flew, the seats were comfortable and the flight attendants treated us all like we were special." She squirmed as if to make her point. "Now they pack us in like cattle."

The preflight announcements started, and the speaker right above their heads drowned out any attempts at further conversation, so Michael sat back and listened. The plane began to pull away from the gate, and the flight attendants went through their safety briefing, then they took their seats, the engines revved, and the plane picked up speed, lifting into the air. Michael hadn't realized he was clutching the arms of his seat until he heard Ruthie say to him, "Are you okay? You look really white."

"I'm okay," Michael answered, uncurling his fingers from the seat and reminding himself to breathe. "I haven't flown in a while, and I sort of forgot what it was like." Michael took a very deep breath, letting it out slowly before taking another. His head stopped swimming, and the feeling he was going to be sick dissipated. His stomach still felt like it had been left on the ground, but he was hoping it would pass.

"If you say so, dear," Ruthie told him as she patted his hand. "I've flown plenty of times, and I used to be afraid too. Then I found something that really helped." She stopped for dramatic effect. "Booze." She smiled and Michael began to laugh. "It didn't really work, but after a while, I just didn't care anymore." She was laughing now, too, and Michael felt better, lapsing back into silence as the beverage carts were wheeled down the aisles. A youngish flight attendant stopped near their row.

"Would you like anything to drink?" he asked, looking twice at Michael.

"A little ginger ale, please," he said, hoping it would settle his stomach, and the attendant placed an opened can and a glass of ice on his tray table with a wink before serving Ruthie and moving on.

"My," Ruthie said from next to him, once the flight attendant had gone. "I wish I could turn young men's heads like that. I used to, you know."

Michael smiled as she looked over at him, and he sipped his soda. "I don't doubt it." Michael felt the soda calming his stomach, and he rested his head back on the seat, closing his eyes, trying to settle both his body and mind. It seemed to work, because he drifted into a place sort of between asleep and awake, just floating as things happened around him, but he didn't pay any attention.

*Mikey.* For a second he thought he heard Devon's voice. Starting forward, he peered around him, looking for Devon, but he was on the plane, and the sound of the engines and people around him stripped away the illusion.

"Are you okay, dear?" Ruthie asked quietly. "They're about to bring around dinner, such as it is." She tapped his hand. "Did something happen? In your sleep you said something like 'Devon'."

"I did," Michael said softly. "I'm sorry." He really hadn't wanted to bring that up. Michael found that Devon was in the back of his mind almost constantly, as was the sense of loss.

"Did he break your heart?"

"Sort of, I guess." Michael wasn't sure what he felt right now. "I'm going to be working in the Netherlands for the next few months, and Devon decided I was going to be gone too much for him." He didn't feel like going into the details. "It came as a bit of a surprise." That was an understatement.

"Breakups always do," Ruthie said, as the flight attendant set a tray down in front of each of them. "Somehow I don't think this Devon was the love of your life," Ruthie commented as she peered over her tray. "Because if he were, you'd be even more upset about him."

"I cared for him," Michael said defensively.

"You probably did, but did you love him?" Ruthie looked up at him innocently with her wrinkled face and a definite wisdom in her overly made-up eyes. "I dated a man when I was younger than you. He was really something—dark eyes, tall, handsome as the day is long, and he could kiss like nobody's business." Ruthie smiled like she was remembering and being naughty at the same time. "We dated for a few months until my father threatened to put an end to it."

"Did you break up with him?"

Ruthie shook her head, pulling the foil off part of her dinner, clicking her teeth. Obviously Ruthie's dinner didn't look any better to her than his own, which was beginning to make his stomach queasy again. "Goodness, no," Ruthie said as her face got that naughty look again. "I saw him for the next month by sneaking out when my folks thought I was at a friend's. I suppose I'm lucky I didn't end up as a 'fallen woman', but he was way too much fun. No, actually, he ended it when he found out that one of my friends would give him something I wouldn't." She raised her eyebrows, making sure Michael knew what she was talking about.

"I bet it hurt," Michael said.

"I was devastated, but my parents didn't know, so I hurt in silence for a while. I met my Daniel a few weeks after that, and Mr. Handsome was a distant memory real fast. If you didn't love this Devon, then it was best to let him go. You'll meet someone better, someone you can love." She picked up her roll and sniffed it, breaking it apart and nibbling on a bit of it before putting it back down with a shake of her head. "We're going to Europe, and they feed us the worst crap imaginable. You'd think they'd have picked up some decent food on their last return trip." Picking up her fork, she ate a bit of the salad while Michael ate some of his and waited to see what his stomach's reaction would be. "Where was I?" Ruthie asked once she swallowed. "Oh, yes. Have you ever been in love, Michael?" She looked at him the way his grandmother had when he was a child and he'd done something she thought he should learn from.

"No, I guess I haven't. Mostly I've worked hard since college and really didn't have time for dating. I met Devon about seven months ago, and he sort of pulled me out of my shell. He was fun, sweet, and we always had a good time." Michael took another bite of his dinner, his stomach not rebelling against the food. "But no, I didn't love him. I should have been able to, though. Devon was everything I could really want in a boyfriend, and I never loved him. I don't know why I didn't." *And Devon deserved to be with someone who loved him.* Michael swallowed hard, staring at the tray of food he suddenly had no desire to touch as his stomach did another loop, but this one wasn't the result of the plane. "I should have loved him and I didn't."

"You can't make yourself love someone. And if Devon left you, then he probably wasn't in love with you, either, because let me tell you, if I was in love with a dish like you, I'd hold on so tight, you'd have finger marks on your...." Ruthie giggled. "You get the picture."

The flight attendant came by, and Ruthie had him take her tray before fishing at her feet for her bag. Michael helped her lift it onto her lap, and she rummaged around inside it, pulling out a cold pack and getting out two plastic containers. "I always carry some of my own food, just in case." Opening the containers, she set them on her tray table, and the aromas made Michael's stomach jump and his appetite return. It was definitely better than the food in front of him. "It's my homemade chicken salad and"—she opened the other container—"macaroni salad. Would you like some? I have plenty."

Michael finished eating his salad, and Ruthie filled the small container. "Thank you," he said, his mouth watering as he took the first bite.

"Daniel always said he fell in love with me the first time I cooked dinner for him. He died almost ten years ago, and I still miss him," she said to introduce the subject, proceeding to tell Michael all about her late husband as Michael ate and listened. The flight attendant took his tray, and the lights in the cabin dimmed for the night portion of the flight. He and Ruthie kept talking for most of the flight. At one point, they both tried to sleep, but it didn't seem to work for either of them, and they continued talking through an equally thrilling breakfast. Unfortunately for both of them, Ruthie did not have omelets stuffed in her bag, and they had to make do with the airline food. Once the breakfast dishes were cleared, the cabin was prepared for arrival, and the plane touched down in Amsterdam.

The plane taxied to the gate, and Michael peered out the windows, hoping to see something, but other than flat land, there wasn't much to see. The Jetway was brought up and the doors opened. Michael helped Ruthie with her bags and received a hug from the lady in return. "You have a good trip, and don't let Devon worry you. You both deserve to be happy." The mischievous look was back for just a second. "You might actually meet one of those tall, dark, and handsome Europeans, and if you do, have fun, young man." She patted his arm and Michael stepped aside, letting Ruthie exit first.

Leaving the plane, he walked with Ruthie through the nearly empty halls and down to passport control. After waiting in line, he handed his passport and paperwork to the officer, who looked him over and stamped his passport before saying something he didn't understand but assumed meant "move on." Taking his paper, Michael followed everyone else to one of the luggage carousels and found Ruthie waiting for her bags, as well. Michael paced nervously, wondering if his luggage had made the transfer like it was supposed to, and he breathed a sigh of relief when it came down the chute. "Do you need me to wait for you?" he asked Ruthie.

"No, I'm fine," she answered, indicating her suitcase, and Michael lifted it off the belt and onto her luggage cart. "Thank you for your help."

"You're welcome," he answered as she pushed her cart toward customs. Michael did the same and found himself in the busy main arrivals terminal where people were meeting each other, hugging before moving away.

His contact at the office, Obed, had told him not to change money, but to get cash from an ATM. Somehow he actually managed to find one and got a couple hundred Euros. Obed had also told him to take a taxi to the hotel and that he would pick him up in the morning to take him to the office. It seemed they already had a car he could use there. Making his way out of the terminal, he stood in line at a sign for the taxis, and when his turn came, Michael told the driver where he needed to go and settled in the backseat of a very comfortable Mercedes.

Obed had told him approximately how much it would cost, and as expected, a hundred-Euro cab ride saw him to the doorway of the Hotel Vianen, and Michael had never been so happy to see a hotel in his life. Taking the elevator upstairs, he found the front desk and checked in, the woman giving him his key and clear directions to what had to be the farthest reaches of the hotel. Once at his room, Michael looked around and barely comprehended anything as he collapsed onto the bed, almost instantly falling asleep.

He woke a few hours later, a little cold, the bedspread tangled around him. He knew he shouldn't sleep too much or he'd never get used to the time change, so he got up, realizing it was about lunchtime here. Figuring he'd take a shower before eating, he went into the bathroom, which seemed almost palatial with its marble floors and counters... and no shower, just a bathtub. Too tired and grungy to care, Michael started the water, returning to the other room to open his suitcase and get out his kit.

Half an hour later, cleaned up, shaved, and feeling half human again, Michael waited at the entrance to the hotel's large restaurant as a man in a dark suit greeted him. "I'm sorry, do you speak English?"

"Of course," the man answered, leading Michael to a table. "Is someone joining you?"

"No. It's just me." Michael sat in the chair he indicated, taking the menu and looking around the room. Everything looked different, more elegant and definitely sort of special, from the tablecloths to the fresh flowers everywhere. Michael opened the menu and couldn't read a word. His first thought was to leave, but he was hungry even if he wasn't sure how he was going to order. A server approached his table, firing off rapid Dutch, and Michael blinked at him. "I'm sorry, I don't understand."

"Oh, English," the server said with a smile. "Would you like an English menu?" A wave of relief washed over Michael, and the server took his menu, returning with an English translation.

"Could I get a glass of water?"

"Of course," he answered moving away. Michael studied the menu carefully, trying to decide what he wanted.

"Excuse me."

Michael put down his menu, looking up at the man standing near his table. "I probably sound wrong, but are you with Shoe Box?"

"Yes." Michael brightened. "I'm Michael Dougherty."

"Stephan Van Der Spoel," he said, holding out his hand. "I work in the marketing department, and Obed told me someone was flying in. Are you alone?"

"Yes, I just arrived a few hours ago. Would you like to join me?"

"I don't want to intrude," Stephan answered.

"You're not, believe me," Michael said, feeling totally relieved for the company and someone who could help him with the menu. Even the English one wasn't particularly helpful. "I'm kind of lost and could certainly use a little help."

Stephan flagged down a waiter, and they spoke back and forth. Stephan went to the table where he'd been seated and returned with his drink, sitting in the chair across from Michael. "Is this your first time here?"

"This is my first time anywhere. I've barely been outside the US before."

"And everything is a bit strange?" Stephan finished for him with a raised eyebrow.

"Yeah, I guess you could put it that way." Michael set down his menu, and Stephan helped by explaining what things really were. When the waiter returned, Michael placed his order with a better idea of what he was going to get. Stephan ordered as well. "Do you eat here often?" It seemed sort of strange to Michael for Stephan to be eating in a hotel restaurant like this.

"I came in to the office to get caught up on some work and did not feel like cooking. Since it is Sunday and there is not much open, I came here to eat. There is a snack bar in town, but they only have fried food, and I wanted something better," Stephan explained as the server brought small bowls of salad for each of them.

"Things seem to be different here," Michael said before tasting the salad. It was good, sort of tangy. "Back home almost everything is open on Sundays."

"People do not spend the day with their families?" Stephan asked before finishing his salad, then setting the bowl aside. "Except areas where tourists go, most businesses are closed on Sunday so workers can spend the day with their families."

"Is that what you'll do after lunch?" Michael asked, feeling the loss of Stephan's company.

Stephan shook his head. "My family lives in the north, and it is too far to go today. After lunch I was going to go home and watch a movie or read."

Their server brought their orders and placed a number of small bowls on the table containing various vegetables and potatoes, obviously for both of them. "This is normal Dutch service," Stephan explained before adding some of the potatoes and vegetables to his plate. Michael did the same and began to eat, his appetite really kicking in as the food hit his stomach. Everything tasted really good, and Michael ate until he thought he would burst. He and Stephan talked while they ate, and Michael was very grateful for the company.

"Is the office near here?" Michael asked once they had finished eating.

"It is on the other side of Vianen in a business park. Do you need a ride, or did you rent a car? I could drive you if you need a ride."

"Obed said he would meet me outside the lobby in the morning. But thank you." Michael smiled and noticed that Stephan did as well, and his gaze didn't drop away. Michael continued smiling until he realized he hadn't been looked at that way since he'd first met Devon. Michael didn't know if Stephan was gay, and it didn't really matter. He'd just broken up with Devon, but it sure felt nice to be looked at like that.

The server left the check, and Michael picked it up, signing the bill to his room. "You do not need to leave a tip," Stephan told him, "service is included in the meal."

"Oh," Michael said as he filled in the amount, "thank you." They got up and walked toward the dining room entrance.

"The town is a small walk that way. I could show it to you if you like," Stephan said a little shyly.

"That would be really nice. I just need to get a jacket. Should I meet you here?" Stephan agreed and Michael hurried back to his room, grabbing his jacket and a sweatshirt from his suitcase before heading back to the lobby. Stephan was still waiting, and they left the hotel. The first thing that Michael noticed was the cool, damp air and overcast skies. Glad he had put on the sweatshirt, Michael followed Stephan along a paved footpath that wound along the edges of people's yards and across a canal. "Do all the houses have yards like these? Every house seems to be surrounded by flowers."

"That is part of being Dutch," Stephan explained. "Yards are very small because land costs a lot. Most people take very good care of their houses and spend a lot of time outdoors in the summer." As they walked by one of the canals, Michael stopped to watch a fountain where it shot water into the air near one of the streets. "These are decorative and keep the water from smelling." Michael nodded and they continued on. "Over there is the grocery store and a bank, as well as a pharmacist." Stephan pointed ahead of them, saying, "The town itself in just down that street."

Stephan led them down a narrow street that opened into a wide area with buildings on either side and parking down the middle. The entire area was paved in stones that looked like they had been there for centuries, as did most of the buildings. "Is this the center of town?" Michael asked as he looked around. The church at the far end of town looked like it had been standing forever. To Michael, the town looked almost like a movie set.

"That's the town hall," Stephan said, pointing to one of the larger buildings. "I'm not sure how old it is exactly, but I would guess it is from the 1600s. The gate at the far end of town is from the 1400s." Stephan explained what many of the stores were as they walked down the main street. "This is the snack bar, and those are clothing shops." They walked past what looked like an antique store with clocks in the window. There appeared to be a lot of small businesses, including a florist and a pizza parlor. Most of them were closed up tight, but there appeared to be plenty of people out for an afternoon walk.

"Do the stores remain open in the evenings?"

"Vianen's late night is Friday. Then the stores stay open until eight. In Utrecht, the late night is Thursday. I could show you, if you like. Utrecht is a large city with a big shopping area and good restaurants."

"That would be great. I've never seen anything like this, and I really want to see it all." Michael felt overwhelmed by this small town that had more history than anything he'd ever seen before. "Does the snack bar have ice cream?"

Stephan chuckled and headed across the street, dodging a few cars as they walked to the snack bar. Inside, people sat around small tables eating out of plastic containers. The place smelled heavenly.

Most of the food appeared to be fried, but the scents were like nothing Michael had ever experienced. It didn't smell like frying grease, but like food, real food with real spices. Wandering around, he peered into a case, wondering what most of the items were, watching as the man behind the counter took stuff out of the case to prepare it. "You need to come here some afternoon and try things," Stephan suggested from behind him. "Everything is quintessentially Dutch. Like Kipkorns and croquettes. Some of them are definitely an acquired taste," Stephan added softly, and they both chuckled. "You wanted ice cream," Stephan reminded him before leading him to the freezer case.

Of course, he could read nothing, and when the counter attendant approached, Michael pointed to something red, hoping it was fruit-flavored. He wasn't disappointed, although it tasted like no fruit he'd had before, tangy and slightly sweet at the same time. Stephan asked for one of the colorful ice creams for himself. Michael insisted on paying, handing the register lady a twenty before stuffing his change in his pocket and then following Stephan out of the shop to a small table on the sidewalk.

"How long do you think you'll be here?" Stephan asked between licks on his cone.

"My project isn't expected to be done until October, so I should be here at least until then." Michael's nervousness had dissipated, as had his out-of-sorts feeling, replaced by a twinge of excitement.

"That must be hard on your family. I'm sorry," he added quickly, "I should not ask such a private question." Stephan seemed embarrassed and would no longer meet his eyes.

"It's not, really. My parents live in Grand Rapids, Michigan, and I live in Central Pennsylvania, so I only see them a few times a year. We talk on the phone regularly, but it doesn't make much difference if I'm here or at home since I won't see them until Christmas, regardless. The hard part is that I know very few people here and only those at the office. In Pennsylvania, I have friends and—" Michael was about to say a boyfriend, but stopped himself. That wasn't true anymore, and he really didn't need to come out to Stephan. He'd read that the Dutch were very accepting, but that didn't mean they all were, and he didn't want to alienate the first person he'd met.

"It is hard to leave home. Where my family lives, there are few jobs, so I moved to Amsterdam after school and then got a job with Shoe Box, so I moved to Vianen. It is near the office and small, like where my family lives." Stephan finished the last of his ice cream, placing the paper wrapper in the trash nearby.

"Did you learn English in school? You speak it very well," Michael complimented, not daring to try to pronounce any of the Dutch words he'd seen on signs. They seemed almost unpronounceable.

"Everyone learns English in school, and most of us speak it in the office because many of the people are from America or from other countries, and English is the language everybody knows." Stephan stood up and Michael followed, wondering if he was going to show him something else, but they seemed headed back the way they came. "You are probably tired, and I must get to the office to finish my work," Stephan explained as they walked back along the path to the hotel. Michael continued taking everything in until they approached the front door.

"Thank you, Stephan, I appreciate you showing me around." Michael extended his hand, and Stephan shook it, seeming to hold it just a little longer than normal. In the States, Michael knew his friends would tell him that meant Stephan was interested in him, but here he figured it was just a cultural thing and let it go.

"It was nice meeting you too," Stephan told him with a warm smile. "I will see you at the office. Maybe we can eat lunch?"

"I'd like that," Michael replied before saying good-bye and turning to go inside. Still smiling, he made his way to his room, where he watched one of the English channels on television for a while until it was time for dinner. He ate in the hotel dining room again, this time sitting by himself, listening to the sound of all the conversations around him. Eating alone, Michael realized that this was how it would be for most of the next five months, and he couldn't say he was really looking forward to it, but he was here, and he decided he was going to make the best of it.

After dinner, he returned to his room, booting up his computer and logging in to the corporate network to check his e-mail and send one to Curtis to let him know he'd arrived. He really didn't have a lot to do, but he was already tired, so he turned off the computer, got ready for bed, and climbed beneath the covers.

He'd just started to doze off when his cell phone rang. "Hello," he said, picking it up off the bedside table, thankful he'd remembered to switch his phone to work in Europe.

"Mikey, it's Devon. I just wanted to make sure you made it." He sounded sad and tentative.

"Hey, Devon," he said, falling back into his usual comfortable tone without even realizing it. "I made it just fine and was about to go to bed."

"I didn't mean to wake you. I just wanted to make sure you were okay." Devon's concern seemed genuine to Michael.

"I'm fine. A little tired and out of sorts, but I'll be fine." Michael listened, but Devon didn't say anything more, and as the silence drew on, he started feeling uncomfortable. "What is it, Devon?"

"I'm sorry, Michael," Devon said, and Michael thought he might have been crying. "I really should have talked to you sooner. It wasn't fair to tell you on the way to the airport." Yeah, Devon was crying; Michael could hear the slight sniffles. "You didn't do anything wrong, and I wish I could tell you why, but I can't."

"Devon." Michael kept his voice calm. "Did you love me? Were you in love with me?"

"You were really kind and thoughtful, Michael. I should have loved you," Devon answered, still sniffling slightly.

"Then I think you have your answer. It's okay, Devon. I don't think we were meant to be the love of each other's lives. You were kind and thoughtful, too, and someone I care about, but I don't think I was in love with you, either. I had plenty of time to think things over on the plane." He left out the part about Ruthie—Devon would not understand. Hell, Michael barely did, but she seemed to really have helped him. "And I think that may be it. Me leaving to work here was probably just what brought it about."

"Then you're not mad?" Devon sounded so young right then, and it brought home the fact that Devon was only twenty-three and he was approaching thirty. Most of the time that hadn't been an issue, but then again maybe it had and they hadn't seen it.

"No. I'm upset and feeling down because I miss you and we had a good time together. You were always a lot of fun and could liven up any place in just a few minutes. I think that's one of the things I like most about you. I'm serious and you're fun."

"Then you'll be okay?" Devon asked, the sniffles gone now.

"Yes. Will you?" Michael countered with a slight smile. They couldn't have been too bad for each other if they were still concerned about each other's feelings. Maybe this was good for both of them.

"I think so. I've never really broken up with someone before. It feels weird. I mean, we know each other pretty well, and it feels strange that I won't be calling you to see how you're doing or looking forward to having dinner or going to a movie."

"We can still do those things. We probably won't go back to my place or your place and drop into bed afterward. But I think we can live with that. Don't you?"

"You want to be friends?" Devon asked, sounding surprised.

"Sure. Why couldn't we be friends? When we weren't dating, we became friends anyway," Michael said before yawning and moving the phone away so Devon wouldn't hear him. "I'll call you when I'm back in town, and maybe we can get together with some other friends and go out or something."

"That would be cool," Devon said, and Michael could hear the relief in his voice, at the same time admitting to himself he felt a bit of the same thing. "Is it okay if I call you sometime?"

"Sure, Devon. I'll talk to you later." Hanging up the phone, Michael rested his head back on the pillow, listening to the sounds of the hotel as he drifted to sleep feeling a little less alone. Talking to Devon had resolved some things, and he might have made a new friend in Stephan. Now all he needed to do was get settled in and his project under way.

# CHAPTER
## Three

MICHAEL woke feeling a little out of sorts—fairly rested but definitely nervous. He cleaned up and brought his computer bag with him to the dining room, where he had some coffee and a bit of fruit. He wasn't really hungry and didn't have much time, either, not wanting to be late for his ride. After signing the check to charge the food to his room, Michael pulled on his suit jacket and grabbed his bag, heading downstairs to wait.

"Michael," a tall, black-haired man called as he approached. "I'm Obed," he added with a grin.

"I knew as soon as I heard your voice," Michael said with a smile. "I've talked to you so many times on the phone."

"I know. It's like we already know each other, but we only now get to meet." Obed shook his hand and led him to his car. "I confirmed on Friday that they do have a car for you. Connell will stop by this morning to bring you the keys."

"Is there anything I should know about driving here?" Michael asked, definitely nervous about driving in a foreign country. All the guys in the office had spent the last week telling him every horror story they could think of.

"No. It's much like driving in the States, except in Amsterdam. Just take the train there. They drive like idiots."

"Thanks, I'll remember that," Michael said as he closed his door and waited for Obed, who started the car and pulled out of the hotel parking lot, giving Michael a rundown on where they were going and how to easily get from the office to the hotel.

"At the office I have a map of the area that you can have, and I think we have some Nederlands maps too. But if you need directions, just ask. I'll help you." Obed kept looking over at him as they drove. "There's nothing to be worried about. Everyone here wants Shoe Finder to be a success, so everyone will help."

"I'm not worried about that as much as finding my way around. It was hard enough at the restaurant in the hotel, let alone when you don't understand any of the signs."

"You will figure it out. It's an adventure, yes?"

Michael chuckled. "That's as good a way to look at it as any." Obed turned off the road, weaving around office buildings, and parked in front of a nondescript square building before getting out of the car. Michael looked around and followed Obed to what looked like the main doors. Obed scanned his badge, and the doors slid open so they could enter.

"Later this morning, I'll take you to HR so they can get you a badge and parking pass," Obed told him as they made their way down a hallway and up the stairs. "This is the IT area, and we have an extra office all set up for you."

Michael unpacked his computer, plugging it in the adapter he'd brought.

"Morning."

He looked up and saw a large man with a huge smile on his face.

"I'm Greg Korick," he said with a slight South African accent.

Michael stood up, shaking the man's hand. Greg was the head of information systems in Europe, and like Obed, Michael had talked to him on the phone many times, but had never met him face to face before. "If you have a minute, I can show you around."

"That'd be great," Michael answered, following Greg down the hallway.

"This is the coffee machine—help yourself. The restrooms are right there." They continued and Michael met a myriad of people whose names he tried to keep straight, but there were simply too many. "Don't worry. There won't be a quiz on everyone's names." Greg led him out of IT and into other areas of the building. "You'll be working with marketing," Greg explained as they walked through another department and up to a large corner office. "Kai," Greg said as he walked right in, "this is Michael Dougherty. He's here for the shoe-locator project."

"Excellent," he said, standing up and walking from behind his desk to shake hands. "Kai Eriksen. It's good to meet you. We've already been talking about branding the new service. It's going to be a pleasure to work with you." Kai led them out of his office and up to a desk. "Stephan will be the member of my team working with you."

Michael smiled when Stephan appeared from behind the wall of one of the cubicles. "Morning, Stephan."

"Good morning, Michael. Did you sleep well?"

"Yes, I think the ice cream was just what I needed." They shared another smile, and for a second, Michael forgot where he was as Stephan's intense dark eyes met his. Michael blinked himself back to reality, wondering exactly what he thought he was doing. "Stephan and I met at the hotel yesterday, and he showed me around town a bit," Michael explained to Kai and Greg as he continued glancing at the handsome man. Neither Greg nor Kai seemed to notice, and Michael returned to the topic at hand. "I'll be setting up a meeting later this week to get all the parties together."

"Great," Stephan answered, "I'm looking forward to it." That could be taken so many ways, but Stephan couldn't possibly mean it in any way other than business. Saying good-byes and shaking hands once again, Michael and Greg moved through additional introductions in other departments to the point where his head was totally swimming by the time he got back to his office.

Taking a few minutes to think, Michael opened his project-plan files on his computer and got to work. Since he'd inherited this project from Kyle, Michael had spent hours getting all the documentation up to his standards, with only the anticipated project timeline to go. Kyle hadn't done much with it, and Michael needed to get it drafted so he could see where the potential schedule and resource conflicts were.

Michael worked, head down, for hours, completely losing track of time. A soft knock on the door pulled his attention away from his computer, and he saw Stephan standing in his doorway. "I don't mean to disturb you, but are you ready for lunch?"

"Yes. Thank you." Michael saved all his files before standing up, working a kink out of his back. "I was wondering how I was going to find the lunchroom in this maze."

"It's in the other building," Stephan explained, leading him down the stairs, outside, and around to the front of the next building in the complex. "They are going to build a connection between the buildings, hopefully before winter." They entered the much newer building, and Stephan led him to the third floor and into a small but well-appointed cafeteria, where they got in line. "They have sandwiches and a daily special," Stephan explained as they got closer.

"Would you get me what you're having?" Michael asked, having no idea what to order, even though he had no idea what the special was. It looked like chicken with some sort of brown sauce, but other than that, he had no idea. Stephan placed their orders, and Michael grabbed a can of diet soda from a case and waited until Stephan set a plate on his tray piled with rice and covered in the brown sauce.

"It's chicken in an Indonesian peanut sauce," Stephan explained as they looked for a place to sit. Greg waved them over, and they sat with him and Obed.

"You were adventurous," Obed commented, and Michael looked at him quizzically, not sure what he meant. "You got the satay," he clarified.

"Stephan got it for me. I figure while I'm here, I'll try some of everything," Michael answered, tasting the rice. The sauce wasn't bad, a little sweet and heavy, but not bad, and he began to eat while the others talked.

"I have to go to the warehouse on Friday," Obed told him from across the table. "Would you like to go with me? It would be a chance for you to meet the team there."

"That would be great," Michael answered. "I don't have anything planned for that day." Obed nodded and the table conversation flowed again, some in English and some in Dutch. Occasionally someone would ask him a question, but mostly he just sat and listened, getting his thoughts together for his afternoon's work. Once he was finished eating, they walked back to the other building as a group, with everyone heading off to their offices. Michael looked for Stephan to thank him for his help, but he'd already returned to work, so Michael did the same, walking to his office and getting back to his plans.

By midafternoon, Michael had finished what he could, finding plenty of questions that needed answers before he could finish. Checking the clock, he picked up the phone, figuring he should call Curtis.

"Michael, just a minute," Curtis said when he answered the phone, and Michael heard him talking to someone else in low tones. "I see you made it okay."

"Yeah. Flights were on time. It wasn't too big a deal," Michael answered, his stomach fluttering the way it always did when he talked to his boss. Curtis had a way of putting his nerves on edge. The sound of keys clicking came through the speaker phone. That was another thing that drove him crazy. Curtis hated being on speaker phone, but used it all the time with his calls.

"I had a conversation with Kyle this morning. He ran into a problem with the Canadian project you turned over to him." Curtis kept talking as he typed. "It seems you missed a number of requirements, and the project is going to be delayed by six months because of it."

"What requirements?" Michael asked. The users had reviewed and signed off on the requirements months ago. Curtis told him, and Michael had to take a minute to think. "Those were discussed with the users and were deemed out of scope." Michael pulled up the project documentation. "If you look at the bottom of the requirements document, you'll see it's documented and signed off."

"Well, it looks like they've changed their minds," Curtis quipped, like that was his fault. Michael wanted to say that Curtis and Kyle needed to do a better job of managing users' expectations, but kept his mouth shut. Curtis could say what he wanted, but Michael had documentation and approvals. He was covered, at least for this one. "And it's going to cost us a six-month delay," Curtis added, his voice becoming louder. "You should have thought of this."

"I did. That's why I documented it and got it signed off," Michael replied, knowing he probably should have said nothing. Curtis was never reasonable when he was like this.

"Mark isn't particularly happy about this, either," Curtis went on, and Michael said nothing, letting his boss ramble. There was nothing he could do or say until Curtis ran out of energy. "Get with Kyle and see if you can help him figure this out. Is there anything else?" Thankfully there was not, and Michael hung up, wondering what the hell crawled up his weasel of a boss's butt. Doing what he was told, Michael called Kyle.

"I heard there was a problem with Canada," Michael said, trying to hide his nerves. He hated that Curtis could do this to him and always tried his best to hide it.

"Yeah. They're insisting on a number of changes. I told them it was a scope change and would delay the project six months, and they said you'd told them it was included in the project."

"It wasn't and they signed off on it."

"I know. They want what they want, and they're trying to bully their way into getting it. You documented it and they signed off on it. It's not your fault, and I told that to Curtis. What's he got you calling me for? I told them that if they wanted the changes, it would result in a six-month delay, and they approved it. I'm sending out the scope change today."

"I wish I knew," Michael said, more concerned about what Mark thought than Curtis. "Sometimes...." Michael stopped himself from saying anything more. He had no idea how much of this conversation would get back to Curtis, and he didn't want to say anything he would need to eat crow for. "It sounds like you have it handled. Let me know if you have any questions. I'll help where I can."

"Thanks, Michael," Kyle said, his voice sounding genuine. "But you've undoubtedly got your hands full there." Kyle stopped and Michael waited. "I just closed my door. I don't know what's going on, but be careful and cover your ass. It's what everyone's doing right now. Sales aren't really good, and Mark's been an absolute bear. He yelled at Sarah in the morning meeting, and she's been his pet director forever."

"Thanks for the warning," Michael said before saying good-bye and hanging up. He didn't know what was wrong with Curtis, or what in particular he had against Michael, but something was up, and he needed this project to go well, and he needed to keep out of the line of fire.

"Do you have a meeting?" Michael saw Obed standing in his doorway. "If you've got a few minutes, I could take you up to HR and get you a badge so you can get in the building tomorrow, and Connell asked me to bring you by afterwards so he can set you up with a car."

"Cool." Michael saved his files, locking his computer before getting up and following Obed upstairs. The HR department was right above where he'd been working, and they got him a badge and access to the building systems in case he needed to come to the office after hours. Leaving there, they found Connell at his desk.

After introductions, he jumped up and led them out of the building to the back parking lot. "I have this car for you." He led Michael to a midnight-blue BMW sedan. "You can use it for the duration of your stay. I also have a gas card for you. This will direct bill your gas to the company. I always tell everyone to watch your speed—they use cameras, and the company doesn't pay speeding tickets. They send them to me, and I pass them on to you." Connell opened the driver's door. "I should have asked if you can drive a standard transmission."

"Yes. My dad made me learn on one, so it's no problem."

"Then you're all set. I have an extra set of keys just in case you need them." Connell leaned into the car and opened the glove compartment. "All the paperwork is in the glove box, should you need it."

Connell handed him the keys, and Michael did his best not to be impressed. At home he drove a small car that was very nearly on its last legs, and here he was being given the use of a BMW with leather seats and God knew what else. "Is your phone Bluetooth enabled?" Connell asked, and Michael fished it out of his pocket. "I'll program it into the car and get it back to you in a little while."

"Thank you so much," Michael said, very excited and a little apprehensive. He'd never had a car this expensive before. "Do I need to arrange for maintenance or anything?"

"You shouldn't. The car was just serviced, and it will tell you if you need anything. If it does, just let me know, and I'll get it taken care of, no problem," Connell said before getting in the car. "I'll bring your phone up to you as soon as I finish here."

Realizing Obed had left, Michael went back inside and found his way back to his office on his own. Connell returned the phone, and Michael worked the rest of the day, leaving the office when everyone else seemed to go home.

The car handled like a dream, and Michael wondered what it would be like to open it up on the freeway, but drove back to the hotel instead. He didn't know his way around yet, and with his luck, he would get lost and not be able to find his way back. As it was, just the trip from the office to the hotel required four roundabouts and enough winding curves to get him completely turned around. Parking near an entrance closer to his room, Michael grabbed his bag and went inside. The hotel was very quiet, and Michael turned on the television in his room for noise, but had nothing really to do. Wishing he'd brought a book, Michael made a note to ask at the office tomorrow where he could find books in English. After eating dinner in the dining room, he went back to his room and booted up his PC, figuring he might as well get some more work done.

Tired and yawning, Michael closed his files and turned off his laptop. He'd been here a day, and he was already bored. Granted, he needed to do some exploring, and he could do that this weekend because he'd have plenty of time. Placing the computer in his bag, Michael turned off the television before cleaning up and getting ready for bed. Climbing beneath the crisp, clean sheets, Michael found himself staring at the ceiling, unable to sleep. He knew it was up to him to get what he could out of this opportunity, but he could see long, lonely days ahead. The people he was working with seemed nice, and everyone had been helpful so far, answering his completely stupid questions, but they had their own lives and couldn't be expected to entertain him. Rolling onto his side, he tried to silence his mind from replaying the conversation with Curtis, and the fact that he was away from home and his friends.

Everyone always thought this kind of travel was fun, and people back at the office at home had said they were jealous. Michael sighed softly, knowing they were wrong. Right now, he'd rather be home in his own bed, and maybe he could have had Devon with him. Closing his eyes again, he did his best to force his mind to stop running and to let him go to sleep.

# CHAPTER
## *Four*

THE end of his first week in Europe turned out almost exactly as he'd expected, and for some things Michael was grateful. He and Curtis had talked almost every day, though there hadn't been any more yelling, and the whole issue around the Canada project had seemed to melt away. Michael chalked it up to stress on Curtis's part, but continued to be wary even as his project moved ahead, albeit a little slower than he would have liked, but the issue was with the software vendor and out of his control. All he could do was make contingency plans and adjust his timelines while he got the development staff at home and the divisional people here in Europe talking to one another and moving forward on their tasks.

His days were very productive and busy, but the evenings tended to be quiet and a little lonely. Michael had wandered all through Vianen and explored some of the surrounding area. He tried not to go back to his hotel right away in the evenings, and he'd found a few interesting restaurants in town, but basically the things he'd done, he was doing alone, and quite frankly, he was getting a little sick of his own company. There had been great things to see, but there hadn't been anyone to share them with. The one disappointment had been that Stephan had talked about taking him into Utrecht for their late shopping yesterday, but he hadn't been in the office that day, and Michael hadn't been willing to attempt going on his own.

Driving into the office on Friday, he went through the things he needed to do, and thankfully there wasn't much. He and Obed were driving to the warehouse that morning, which was great, because he'd learned through the week that in order to get his project completed, there were a number of things that the warehouse would need to do to help support it, so meeting the team there was going to be very helpful. Pulling into the parking lot, Michael parked and grabbed his bag from the backseat, then walked toward the building.

"Michael." He heard someone call from behind him, and he turned as Stephan hurried to catch up with him. "I apologize for yesterday. I said we could go to Utrecht, but I got called away on a family issue." He didn't elaborate and Michael didn't ask. He'd learned rather quickly that people here were quiet about their private lives. "Would you like to go into Vianen shopping this evening?"

"That would be great," Michael answered. "I'm leaving for the warehouse with Obed in a little while, but we should be back before five." They walked into the building together and continued to Michael's office.

"I could meet you at your hotel, and we could walk into town again if that is okay with you."

"Wonderful. I'll meet you in the lobby. What time?"

"Five thirty? We can look around, and there's a nice restaurant where we can have dinner if you would like." Stephan seemed very tentative.

"Even better," Michael said with a smile as Obed poked his head in the door.

"Will you be ready in fifteen minutes?"

"Yeah," Michael answered, and Obed walked on.

"You are busy, but I will see you tonight at the hotel," Stephan said with a smile before leaving the office.

Michael booted up his laptop and answered his e-mails, nearly groaning when he saw one from Curtis, but thankfully it was just a notification of a team meeting that Michael would get to miss. When he finished going through his messages, Michael shut down his computer just as Obed walked into his office.

"I'm ready when you are," Michael quipped as he slid the laptop into his bag, following Obed out to his car. They drove out of the city and through rural areas that looked untouched by time, to a small industrial park near the German border. Michael spent much of the morning and afternoon in meetings with the IS people at the warehouse, determining how they were going to integrate their systems into the project. They broke for lunch, and then Michael spent the rest of the day writing up what they'd decided and integrating their design decisions into the project documentation. One thing was becoming obvious: this project was more complex and touched more processes than anyone had thought.

By late afternoon, Michael had finished up, and it looked as though Obed had, too, so they started the trip back to the office. "It's beautiful out here," Michael commented as they drove a stretch of freeway that cut through some of the greenest landscape Michael had ever seen.

"The Dutch grow a good percentage of Europe's produce. Some in fields like that and others under hectares and kilometers of glass. The flooding that happens occasionally replenishes the soil and keeps it fertile."

"Is there much to see out in this area of the country?" Michael asked, still enthralled by the landscape passing outside the window. "Are there windmills?"

Obed chuckled. "No, there isn't a lot in this part of the country except farms like you see, and there aren't any windmills around here, either. Those are mostly in the north and closer to the sea. If you want to go up that way, there are people in the office who can tell you where you can find some, though."

"I saw one once when I was a kid," Michael explained. "We visited Holland, Michigan, and I think they purchased one and had it brought over and reassembled. It was pretty interesting, as I remember." He and Obed kept talking, with Obed answering all Michael's questions about whatever they happened to be passing at the time, finally arriving back at the office a little before five. "I'm meeting Stephan from marketing at the hotel in half an hour. We're going to wander around Vianen and then get some dinner. You're welcome to join us if you like."

"No, thank you. My wife is waiting at home, and the kids are probably driving her crazy by now," Obed explained, and Michael got out, grabbing his bag before saying good-bye and heading to his own car for the short trip to the hotel.

Michael hurried to his room and cleaned up a little, changing his shirt before going back to the lobby, where he saw Stephan sitting in one of the chairs. "Are you ready?" Stephan said as he stood up and walked to Michael. "Unfortunately, it's been beautiful all day, but now it feels like rain. Would you like to drive? That way you can learn your way around."

"Sure," Michael said, thankful he'd grabbed his keys out of habit as he left his room. "I saw the most interesting things today, but I suppose they aren't as interesting to you because you see them all the time," Michael commented as they walked out of the hotel to where he'd parked his car. "Houses and churches that looked like they'd been there forever, and fields that looked like they couldn't be real, they were so perfect." Michael unlocked the doors, and Stephan walked to the passenger side, getting in the car.

"That's part of being Dutch, I guess. Land is in short supply, so we're very used to making the most of it and getting everything we can from it," Stephan explained as Michael started the car. "The reason that field looked perfect was probably because it was. Every plant had been tended and nourished to produce as much as possible." Michael listened as he pulled out onto the road with Stephan directing him into the heart of the small town, and to his relief Michael actually found a place to park.

People wandered up and down the street carrying shopping bags and packages. The two of them joined the flow, stopping in almost every store, except the ones that looked like they carried only women's clothes. "Does that mean what I think it does?" Michael asked pointing to a sign that read, "Antik."

"If you mean antiques, then yes. Sophie and Renard are really nice people. He's Dutch, she's French, and they travel all over," Stephan explained as he started across the street. "They don't appear to be open. Perhaps they are on one of their buying trips." They continued walking and browsing, moving steadily toward the far side of town. There didn't appear to be anything either Michael or Stephan needed, but it was certainly nice to have company.

Stephan pointed across the street. "This is the restaurant I was telling you about, De Graaf van Brederode."

"Excellent," Michael responded, following Stephan, definitely hungry and enjoying the company immensely. "What kind of food do they serve?"

"This is a very nice restaurant." Stephan became quiet for a second, as if searching his mind. "Gourmet? Is that the word?"

Michael smiled. "Yes, that's the word, although that kind of food may be a bit lost on me," he commented lightly, holding the door before following Stephan into a small vestibule. They were greeted by an elegant woman in formal evening attire. She spoke to Stephan, and Michael used the time as an opportunity to look around the cleanly designed area and through the glass doors to the understated elegance of the restaurant, wondering just what kind of restaurant this was. Before he could ask anything more, the woman led Stephan through the glass doors, and Michael followed behind. She seated them at a table near the front windows where they could watch everyone walk past.

She said something to Michael.

"I'm sorry, I don't understand," he replied.

"Would you like something from the bar?" she asked in perfect English with only the barest hint of an accent. Michael looked to Stephan, who explained that they would order a bottle of wine once they had made their selections for dinner, and she nodded and handed them each a menu. "I do not have an English menu, but I will be happy to translate or answer any questions for you." He opened the menu and she stood near his shoulder. "These are appetizers," she said, pointing down the list, patiently explaining each dish. "Please take your time to decide." Stephan asked for glasses of water, and she brought them before returning to her station.

"I've never had any of this before, and I'm not sure what to order, but everything sounds so good," Michael said, still staring at the menu he couldn't read, and he decided to sort of take a chance. After a while, their waiter approached to take their orders.

"I'd like to start with the carpaccio, and then the beef with the sauce." Michael pointed to each dish to make sure he was ordering the correct one.

"Béarnaise," the waiter explained. "You will enjoy it very much."

He handed back the menu, and the waiter took Stephan's order. Michael didn't try to determine what Stephan was ordering, but recognized when he selected the bottle of wine. The waiter brought glasses and opened the wine, showing the cork to Stephan before pouring him a taste, and then pouring both glasses once Stephan approved. Michael was just lifting his glass for a taste when his phone beeped softly in his pocket.

"Excuse me a minute, please." Placing his napkin at his place, he walked out to the vestibule before answering the phone. "Hello." He didn't recognize the number, but it appeared to be from the office.

"Michael, it's Curtis, and we're in the conference room with Kyle and the other managers. We just had a meeting with Mark, and he needs the timelines for all the projects first thing Monday morning. I already have them for your other projects, but I need it for Shoe Finder." Obviously the meeting with Mark hadn't gone well because Curtis was as wound up as Michael had ever heard him, talking a mile a minute. "What time is it there, anyway?"

Michael checked his watch. "About eight o'clock at night."

"Oh," Curtis said. "Well, it wasn't as though you had other things to do." Michael didn't know how to respond to that, so said nothing. "I'd like them done by the time I go home tonight so I can review them all over the weekend," he went on to explain.

"Curtis, it's Friday night," Michael explained levelly. "I have some additional work to make sure everything is correct, and then the first cut will be ready. I can send it to you before you get in Monday morning." He heard Curtis huff before agreeing somewhat reluctantly. Then he heard Curtis tell everyone else to leave the room, and he heard a door close.

"We're alone now. Are your timelines really that close?" Curtis asked.

"Of course, I said they were," Michael replied a little testily. He didn't appreciate being called a liar. "I've worked on them all week between meetings," he said as he peered through the glass door, seeing their waiter approaching their table and leaving again. "I'm at dinner. Is there something else you need?"

"No." Then silence.

"Then have a nice weekend, and I'll speak to you on Monday."

"Okay." Curtis sounded like he wanted to ask something, and Michael waited. "Are you out with someone?" He stressed the word out in a strange, inquisitive way that Michael couldn't quite fathom.

"I'm having dinner with one of the guys from the office," Michael supplied, wondering just where Curtis was going. "He's showing me around and helping me get settled."

"Good, because you're there on business, not...." Curtis left the rest unsaid before telling him good-bye. Michael disconnected and shook his head in confusion before walking back into the restaurant, finding his napkin refolded at his place.

"I'm sorry, that was Curtis," Michael explained as he sat back down.

"This late," Stephan commented.

Michael sighed softly, trying to figure out a way to explain. "I don't think he understands time zones—if it's two in the afternoon where he is, then it's two o'clock everywhere," Michael answered, and Stephan looked at him strangely, rolling his eyes. "Sometimes I think he resides in his own little world. I call it Curtisland, where everything is according to Curtis and nothing makes sense at all, at least to anyone else."

Stephan laughed, and Michael was pleased he got the joke. Their server brought the appetizers, placing a large plate in front of him covered in what looked like very thinly sliced red meat with a small salad in the middle. Michael thanked him before trying a little of the salad and then the beef. "Eat them together," Stephan instructed. "It's better that way." Michael did, and the flavor burst on his tongue, and he suppressed a sigh with a sip of wine before returning to the amazing dish. "The meat is raw and raised especially to be eaten that way," Stephan explained, and Michael felt his eyes widen at the thought of eating raw meat, but he didn't let it stop him, not for a second, because it tasted so good.

"May I ask you a private question?"

Michael smiled at Stephan's odd wording, but said nothing. "Certainly."

Stephan set down his fork. "What did your girlfriend think of you working here?"

"I don't have a girlfriend, but my boyfriend wasn't too happy and decided he wanted to see someone else."

"Oh," Stephan replied. "I prefer men too," he added. "I had a boyfriend, as you say, for a while last year, but he moved back to France." Stephan smiled. "I thought you might have been gay, but I was not sure." Stephan picked up his fork, and Michael saw him studying his plate. Michael had been around enough to know what that look meant, at least he hoped he knew what that look meant. They finished their appetizers, and the server took away the dishes. "I am going to Bruges tomorrow with some friends. Would you like to come along? Hans and Johan have friends in from the States, and they are showing them around and asked if I'd like to come."

"I don't want to be in the way," Michael responded, trying to keep the excitement out of his voice.

"You will not. I'd like to show you around. Bruges is a very beautiful city in Belgium with canals and many old buildings," Stephan explained.

Their server brought their entrees, setting a beautifully arranged plate in front of him and an equally impressive one in front of Stephan.

"If you're sure your friends won't mind," Michael said, not wanting to intrude, but interested in seeing the city and spending more time with Stephan, although he cautioned himself against getting his hopes up in the romantic department. He was only in Europe for a few months, so they should probably just remain friends.

"They will not mind," Stephan assured him. "They keep, uh, setting me up with men they know."

Michael nodded. "I understand. I have a friend like that, but he gave up years ago." To Michael's eternal gratitude, that, combined with the fact that David had moved to Florida, saved him from David's disastrous fix-ups. They ate leisurely, talking about the details for the following morning. Stephan told him about Bruges, describing some of the things they were going to see.

"There are many special things, but I want them to be a surprise," Stephan told him with a twinkle in his eyes. They continued talking through dinner, and Michael found himself telling Stephan about his family as well as what Pennsylvania was like. Once dinner was done, Michael checked his watch and realized they'd talked and eaten for two hours, and he wondered where the time had gone. Their server placed the check on the table, and Michael reached for it.

"No, Michael, I must insist," Stephan said.

"Let's say this is an early thank-you for tomorrow." Michael handed his credit card to the server and waited for him to return with the credit-card slip. He left a small tip and signed the slip. He and Stephan got up, thanking the hostess and their server as they left the restaurant. The sidewalks were wet as they walked back to Michael's car, and Stephan directed him down the one-way streets, onto the main road, and back to his hotel. Saying good night, they agreed to meet at seven thirty the following morning. Michael thanked Stephan again for a wonderful evening before walking into the hotel and down to his room.

Booting up his PC, Michael worked for an hour or so before shutting it down again, setting his alarm, and going to bed, looking forward to the morning.

# CHAPTER
## Five

THE alarm sounded and Michael jumped out of bed, looking forward to the day ahead. Peering outside, he was pleased that the rain from the previous day seemed to be gone, the sun shining over the small courtyard outside. After cleaning up and dressing, Michael hurried downstairs for a quick breakfast before returning to his room to get the things he thought he'd need for the day. As he walked out of the hotel, he saw Stephan walking toward him.

"There's a shuttle to the Utrecht train station from the hotel." Stephan pointed to a sign. "It should be here in just a few minutes." Sure enough, a small bus pulled in, and they got on, paying the small fee and sitting down. The ride to the train station didn't take long, and Stephan explained to him where they were going. "This week, I promise, if you want, I will take you to late shopping on Thursday."

"I'd like that," Michael told him as the bus wound through the city streets, pulling into the train station.

"We are meeting my friends on the train platform," Stephan told him as he led them through the station to the ticket office. Stephan helped him buy a train ticket before leading him through the throngs of people and down onto the platform. Stephan looked around and waved to a small group of men before walking over. The men greeted each other with handshakes before Stephan made introductions. "Hans and Johan, this is Michael. Michael, Hans and Johan are old friends."

"This is Peter," Hans said, introducing their companion. "He and his wife Susan are visiting us from Nebraska."

"Susan wasn't feeling well this morning," Peter said, and explained that Susan was pregnant. He went on to explain all the details that every expectant parent knows, but mean very little to someone who figured he had no chance of ever being in his place. Michael listened and nodded at the right places.

"Didn't you want to stay with Susan if she isn't feeling well?" Michael asked, trying not to sound like some kind of asshole.

Hans leaned in as if to share a secret, and said, "I think the only thing Susan's sick of right now is Peter." The guys all laughed, including Peter.

"Our platform is over this way," Stephan explained, and they walked toward the stairs as a group, descending below the station and down to the tracks. Michael found he was quite excited. He'd ridden in trains before, but he'd heard that trains in Europe were different, and he wasn't quite sure what to expect. When the train pulled in, Stephan led them onto one of the cars and then upstairs to a lookout area with windows all around. Everyone took seats in what appeared to be conversation areas with sets of seats facing each other, and soon the train began to move, pulling out of the station and rapidly leaving the city behind.

"Is this your first visit to the Netherlands?" Johan asked. Both Hans and Johan appeared older than Michael, but both men were handsome. They had trim bodies and slightly graying dark hair, and eyes that looked at one another the way Michael hoped someone would one day look at him.

"This is my first visit to Europe," Michael answered, pulling himself out of his examination of the handsome men. "I'm here for almost six months working on a project, and Stephan asked if I'd like to come along today." He couldn't help glancing at his host. "I haven't seen anything yet." Michael tried to keep the excitement out of his voice, not wanting to appear like some wide-eyed kid, but he doubted he was very successful.

"It is funny," Hans observed from where he sat across from Michael, "but we'd never come to Bruges or most any place else if it wasn't for visitors. We went to the South of France a few years ago to relax on the beach, and we've been to Tenerife and Malta, but otherwise we stay close to home." Johan leaned close to Hans, saying something in his lover's ear. Hans smiled before nudging Johan with his shoulder. "Bruges is a wonderful place to fall in love," Hans said, looking at both Stephan and Michael.

"For goodness' sake," Stephan said softly before turning to Michael. "Hans has been trying to, uh, fix me up for a while now." The conversation continued, and Michael found himself staring out the window for a while, watching as the scenery steadily passed by the windows. Cities gave way to towns and farms and then turned back into city as they approached Rotterdam. They had to change trains and soon they were off again. "We're about to cross into Belgium," Stephan explained, and a short time later, they stopped to change engines and then they were on their way.

Everyone continued talking as they continued on, once again changing trains in Antwerp for a smaller train that wound through the Belgian countryside. "Things are different in Belgium," Stephan explained. "The country is larger and has fewer people, so it's wilder, more natural, I guess." They passed through some small towns, and Michael noticed that Peter was equally enthralled by the scenery. The other guys let them marvel at what passed the windows.

"Bruges is coming up soon," Hans explained as the train pulled away from a stop. "We should get ready to exit." They gathered their things, not that there was much, and when the train stopped, they all got off and wandered through the old train station toward the exit. As soon as they got outside, Michael wished he'd brought a heavier jacket. The sun was shining, but the breeze was cool and went through his clothes. "The town center is this direction, and we'll have to walk a short way," Hans instructed.

"We should stop for lunch first," Johan commented from the back of the group, and Hans laughed, saying something about his partner always being hungry.

Michael did his best to keep up with the group, but every time they turned a corner he saw something he'd never seen before: cathedrals, stores in buildings that looked like they had been there forever, and when they came to the square, Michael stopped in his tracks, looking all around him at the decorated buildings. "Michael, are you all right?" Stephan asked when he stopped for what had to be the millionth time.

"I'm fine. I just want to see everything."

"You will, I promise. We're going to have lunch, and then I'll take you all around, and we can take a boat tour of the canals." Michael nodded and shivered slightly when the wind blew through the square. "Are you cold?" Stephan asked, and without waiting, he opened the backpack he'd been carrying and pulled out a sweatshirt. "You can wear this if you want," Stephan told him.

"Won't you need it?" Michael asked, not wanting Stephan to be cold because he'd given him his sweatshirt.

"Probably not. This is perfect outdoor weather," Stephan replied, handing Michael the sweatshirt. Michael pulled it over his head, grateful for the warmth and Stephan's thoughtfulness.

"Would everyone like to sit outside?" Johan asked, walking toward a restaurant on the square. They all agreed. Johan spoke with the maître d', and they were seated immediately at a table right on the square under an awning. Menus were presented, and Michael was relieved to see they were in both Dutch and English, although he forgot about it completely as he watched horse-drawn carriages pass and heard bells ringing the hour across the square.

"Michael," Stephan said quietly from next to him, "do you know what you want?"

Michael had no idea, but took a stab and ordered the schnitzel when it was his turn to order. Food began to appear, and the conversation turned to the day's activities. Peter wanted to go shopping, so after lunch Hans and Johan were going to take Peter walking down the shopping streets. Michael wanted to see things, so he and Stephan were going off on their own.

The food arrived, and Michael took a tentative bite before eating with relish. "It is good, yes?" Stephan asked with a smile.

Michael put down his fork, swallowing before answering, "It's wonderful. I think I found a new favorite food." They all chuckled lightly and continued eating and talking. When they were finished, they paid the bill and left the table, agreeing to meet back at the restaurant later that afternoon.

"Come," Stephan told him. "I have something very special to show you." Stephan had already begun walking, and Michael followed him out of the square and along a busy street to a huge church. "This cathedral is very important," Stephan told him and walked toward the entrance. Michael paid the small entrance fee, and they stepped inside the massive building and toward an altar where people seemed to be congregating, snapping pictures. "That small Madonna and child," Stephan explained, and Michael nodded, "is the only work by Michelangelo outside Italy."

Michael gaped open-mouthed at the small marble sculpture. He could only get so close, but even from the distance everyone was required to stay back, he could see amazing details in the small work. "I heard about things like this but never expected to actually see them." He'd seen pictures in books of famous artworks, but to get to see one for real was amazing. "Is there more?"

"There's lots more," Stephan assured him as they moved away and wandered through the church, with its massive altars and large sculptures of saints, centuries old. "Do you like it?"

"Yes," Michael answered, his head craned back looking up toward the ceiling towering overhead. "It's beautiful."

Stephan chuckled. "There's a lot more to see whenever you are ready." Michael continued exploring, and Stephan patiently went with him. He seemed to be enjoying watching Michael marvel at everything. After a while, they left the church, walking along cobbled streets before getting in a line for the canal tours. "They have these in Amsterdam, too, but they're more fun here, more traditional." When their turn came, they paid and got into a medium-sized wooden boat, and a crew member pushed off from the side of the canal. The small motor rumbled as they went under arched stone bridges and by buildings that the tour guide said were hundreds of years old.

"Thank you for bringing me here," Michael told Stephan when they stepped off the boat and back onto the cobbled street. "It's amazing."

They wandered the streets for a while, taking in the shops, and Michael began looking around for something to drink.

"Are you thirsty?" Stephan asked, almost reading his mind. "We can get a traditional Belgian beer if you like."

"That sounds perfect," Michael answered with a smile, following Stephan to a tavern, where a busty bar maid talked to both of them before bringing huge glasses of whatever beer Stephan had ordered. "Dang, this is good," Michael crooned happily after the first sip of the smooth, cool brew wet his parched throat. "Sure spoils me for the stuff we have back home."

"I've had American beer, once."

"And it's nothing like this," Michael added with a grin, as they toasted before taking another gulp. "Hans, Johan, Peter," Michael called when he saw the other men walk in. They joined Stephan and Michael and ordered beers, the five of them chattering about what they'd seen, and after a second round of beer, they all agreed that they'd better get back to the train station while they still could. Michael figured Stephan and the guys were probably used to it, but he was already feeling a little light-headed, and he figured Peter was too.

The ride back was just the reverse of the trip there. They changed trains at the same places and arrived back in Utrecht as it was just beginning to get dark. Hans, Johan, and Peter said their good-byes after handshakes and waves.

"Are you hungry? There's an unusual African restaurant near the canal," Stephan said.

"Sure," Michael answered, not wanting the day to end. He couldn't remember the last time he'd had so much fun. Stephan was wonderful company. "My treat," Michael insisted, and let Stephan lead them to what appeared to be a deep canal with stairs leading down. They led to an area with spaces cut into the side of the canal, probably originally for storage, but now they housed all kinds of places to eat. The Zebra was one of those places, and to Michael's surprise, the restaurant's namesake was on the menu, along with springbok and gazelle. "I can tell my concepts of food are going to be broadened while I'm here," Michael commented as he looked at the menu.

"Is that good?"

"I think it's very good," Michael answered before ordering the mixed grill, which included a number of different exotic meats. He wasn't quite sure what Stephan ordered, but when their meals came, they each let the other taste. As they ate, the lights came on around the restaurants, tiny fairy lights shining off the water. Michael swept his gaze around, trying to take in everything, but stopped when he saw Stephan looking back at him, brown eyes warm, face indulgently sweet.

"Have you ever seen the sea? I'm planning to go to the beach tomorrow. Would you like to come with me? Most people don't actually go in the water because it's cold, but there's all kinds of things to do."

"I don't want to take you away from your friends," Michael responded cautiously. "I'd love to go with you, but won't I be keeping you from things you have to do?" He wanted to spend time with Stephan, and the thought of spending another day with him sounded like a lot of fun, but he didn't want Stephan to get tired of his company.

"No. I'd planned this trip a long time ago with a friend, but he can't go." Stephan took a small bite of his dinner. "We sort of planned to go as a couple, but we aren't a couple anymore." Stephan looked away and appeared to become very interested in his food.

"How long were you together?" Michael asked. It seemed like the proper thing to say, but he wondered if he should even bring it up at all. Stephan had been happy all day and now he seemed withdrawn and sad.

"About six months, I suppose," Stephan responded. "It does not seem like a long time, but I was in love with him, and I thought he loved me."

"But he left you?" Michael supplied and saw Stephan nod slowly.

"I am…." He paused. "Over him?" When Michael nodded, Stephan continued. "We planned to go to the beach tomorrow because it was going to be our anniversary. I thought I should go anyway to make sure I was done with him, and I think I am, but…."

"It's hard," Michael said. "I understand."

"I guess I should have paid closer attention to Heinrich," Stephan commented with a soft sigh before lapsing into quiet again.

Michael watched his new friend closely, seeing the pain flash on his face. "Is this something you want to talk about? I'll listen if you want."

Stephan smiled slightly, some of the hurt slipping from his face. "I do not want to trouble you with my heartache." Stephan took another bite of his stew before setting down his spoon again. "I cannot talk to my family about Heinrich because they hated him." Stephan stopped again, and Michael said nothing, paying attention to his dinner partner, meeting his eyes. "I...," Stephan stammered, "this is hard to talk about."

Michael nodded his head slowly. He knew it was hard, and to his surprise, Michael realized he hadn't thought of Devon all day. He now understood that their breakup was probably for the best. Devon deserved to be with someone who would make him happy, and while they'd had fun while they were together, Michael couldn't see Devon reacting like Stephan was now over him any more than he could imagine himself feeling hurt for Devon. Focusing on Stephan again, he continued waiting. "I'm here to listen," Michael said softly, surprised at his instinct to want to make Stephan's hurt go away and how badly he wanted to see him smile like he had when they were in Bruges.

"We—" Stephan started to say and then stopped, and it looked like he was at war with himself somehow. "It's hard to talk about things like this with someone outside my family. We're raised that these things are private."

"We're friends, aren't we? And friends help each other. If you don't want to talk about it, I'll understand and respect that. If you want to confide in me, I'll listen and treat it with confidence." Michael knew in his heart that this Heinrich person had hurt Stephan pretty badly, especially if it still hurt this much.

"It's very embarrassing," Stephan murmured to his food and remained quiet. Michael knew the second he'd made up his mind because his head lifted and his expression firmed. "I need to explain that

Heinrich was a really big guy, sort of the Nordic-god type. He looked Scandinavian, but he was German. Part of his family must have come from the far north."

"Big, blond, and beautiful?" Michael commented, and he saw Stephan smile and nod.

"Exactly. And you can add bossy and a bit of a bully, now that I think about it." Stephan's expression hardened. "I met him at work about a year ago, I think. He was in the accounting department, and he seemed to notice me right away." Stephan seemed surprised, but Michael wasn't. Stephan was very handsome with his dark eyes, longish, jet-black hair, and just a touch of olive to his complexion. "He pursued me right away, and I think I was flattered. Heinrich was very handsome, and I couldn't figure why he was interested in me."

Michael furrowed his brow, but kept quiet. Stephan had no reason to be flattered. If anything, this Heinrich should have been flattered that Stephan was willing to give him the time of day. Stephan was a kind person who'd taken his own time to show Michael around and help him begin to find his way in a strange country. No one else in the office had asked or volunteered, not even to join him for dinner, but Stephan had.

"At first I thought he and I were compatible. Heinrich was strong and very in charge," Stephan told him, his cheeks coloring slightly as he once again studied his food, eating again, probably as cover.

Michael felt as though he needed to say something to make Stephan feel better. "You have nothing to be embarrassed about, you know. Everyone has a relationship that seems right at the beginning, but turns out differently once they get to know the person better."

"It wasn't that, exactly. Like I said, Heinrich was in charge, and I liked it that way."

Michael clued in to what Stephan was saying, and his eyes widened in recognition as he squirmed slightly in the chair. Was Stephan saying what he thought he was? "Is that what you like?" Michael asked, his mouth suddenly dry.

"I think so," Stephan replied. "But Heinrich was too aggressive and…." Stephan swallowed and his voice trailed off.

"Did he hurt you?" Michael inquired, suddenly very concerned and surprised at the vehemence in his question. Lowering his voice, he leaned across the table. "Let's finish eating and we can talk somewhere less public, if you want."

Stephan nodded and they ate quietly, neither of them saying much. Michael found himself worrying about Stephan and then wondering why he was so worried and why he felt the way he did about someone he'd met less than a week ago. He tried to explain to himself that Stephan was a friend and that he cared about him as a friend, but he'd had friends before, and he'd never felt his insides turn around and around the way they were at the thought of someone hurting Stephan. Once they were done, Michael paid the bill and they walked back toward the car. Normally, Michael would have been looking all around him, but he was worried about Stephan.

In the car, Michael followed Stephan's directions back to the hotel, and he led the way to his room. Just outside his door was a small, out-of-the-way seating area that no one seemed to use. Michael motioned toward one of the chairs, and Stephan sat down. "I can't believe I'm telling you all this," Stephan said softly.

"You don't have to tell me anything you aren't comfortable with."

Stephan looked up, and Michael felt his heart leap slightly. "That's the surprising part. I feel like I can talk to you." Stephan kept his face neutral. For a second, Michael thought Stephan might be overcome by his emotions, but he kept himself under control. "I told you Heinrich liked to be in control, and he really liked that when it came to things... intimate."

"You like having someone else in charge in the bedroom," Michael clarified, his heart beating just a little faster.

"Yes, and Heinrich liked being in charge, maybe a little too much. Things started out a lot of fun. Heinrich was hot and very sexy. But as time went on, he got more controlling."

"He didn't know when to stop," Michael supplied.

"Exactly, and a few times he went too far and hurt me. I don't think he meant to, but he did. After the last time, I told him he had to back off, and he got angry and dumped me." Stephan obviously didn't want to go into the details, and Michael didn't want to pry. It wasn't his place. "I still kind of like it when...." Stephan stopped, looking out the windows.

"There's nothing wrong with what you want," Michael started to say, trying to find the right words. "There is something wrong with this Heinrich, though. He should have learned and respected your limits. He should never have bullied or made you do anything you weren't comfortable with." God, Michael could remember the time he'd had nearly this same conversation with Devon. Except at the time, Devon had been really excited and barely paid attention, while Stephan had been hurt. "You needed to be able to trust him, and he let you down. It took strength, real strength, to tell him to stop." Michael reached out, intending to touch Stephan's shoulder, but stopped himself, knowing that simple touch would be the start of something Michael wasn't really sure he was ready to begin.

"You understand?" Stephan asked. "I always thought there was something not quite right about me. Heinrich always told me I was wrong...."

Michael sighed as Stephan stopped talking. "He told you what you wanted was sick and twisted and then used that to control you. I'll tell you this much. It was Heinrich who was sick and twisted. Is he still working at the office?"

"No," Stephan answered, looking nervous. "He left a few months ago."

Michael's phone rang, and he fished it out of his pocket. "It's my boss," he told Stephan with an exaggerated sigh, wondering just what he wanted on a Saturday evening. Answering it, Michael felt the nerves in his stomach tighten. Why this man did that to him drove Michael crazy. He was normally a confident person, but Curtis got under his skin every time.

"Michael." Curtis sounded frantic. "I need those plans right away. Mark wants to go over everything on Monday."

"They're almost done. I just need a few estimates from accounting, and the people I need to speak with were out of the office last week.

They're back on Monday, and I'll send you the plans before you get into the office," Michael said levelly. This was the same thing he'd told him earlier, and Curtis had already agreed. This was one of the advantages of being six hours ahead.

"I want to look them over this weekend in case there's anything wrong."

"When have you known my plans to be wrong?" he asked, offended by Curtis's insinuation, and he heard silence on the other end of the line. "They may change based on customer requests, but I always document them very thoroughly."

"I know," Curtis replied, sounding almost contrite. "Monday is fine."

"Is everything okay?" Michael asked, regretting his question almost as soon as he'd asked. Curtis started in on a litany of problems, most of them ridiculously small, but leave it to Curtis to blow them out of proportion. "Let me know if I can help," Michael said when Curtis eventually came up for air.

"Just keep things under control there," Curtis said, and before Michael could answer, he found himself listening to a dead line. Hanging up the phone, he shoved it into his pocket as Stephan got to his feet.

"You probably have work to do, and I don't want to get in your way."

"You aren't. I should get some things done, though. What time would you like to meet in the morning? That is, if your offer to go to the beach is still good." Michael wasn't sure how Stephan would react after their talk. He half expected him to want to put some distance between them after the rather intimate conversation they'd had.

"You will go?"

"Yes, of course. The beach sounds like fun." Michael smiled and then looked down at himself, realizing he was still wearing Stephan's sweatshirt. "I should give this back to you," Michael said as he started to pull it off.

"Keep it. You'll probably need it tomorrow. Even if it's sunny, the wind off the water will be cold." Stephan stopped, and Michael felt as well as saw their eyes meet. He was sorely tempted to see what Stephan's full lips tasted like, but held himself back again. A few seconds later, Stephan turned and stepped away. "I'll pick you up at nine, if that's good."

"I'll be ready," Michael answered as he watched Stephan turn and walk down the hall. Michael's eyes followed him the entire way. He knew he really should not be looking at his friend's butt. Maybe going to the beach tomorrow wasn't a good idea. He was attracted to Stephan, he knew it, but doing anything about it was so not a good idea. For one thing, he was a coworker. Also, Stephan was still getting over a bad relationship, and Michael had just broken up with Devon a week ago. Furthermore, Stephan was a friend, the only one he had here so far, and you didn't screw your friends. He'd learned that one the hard way a few years back, and he wasn't interested in a repeat of that drama. No, as much as he thought the other man attractive, and he certainly was, and as much as he wanted to show Stephan how he should be treated, Michael told himself that they needed to just be friends.

Stepping to his room, Michael opened the door and walked to the table, booting up his PC to get the last of the plans ready to send to Curtis. He tried to work, but his mind really wasn't on it. He kept seeing Stephan's face and kept wondering what he'd look like on his bed, eyes rolling back under his touch. "Stop it," he told himself. There was no guarantee that Stephan was really interested in him, and it wasn't going to happen, anyway. Giving up on work, Michael saved and closed his files before turning on the television. He had to have something to take his mind off Stephan. Luckily, he found one of the BBC channels, and he was able to watch a few shows in English before turning in for the night.

He didn't sleep well at all—it was still dark, and Michael was pacing his room trying to wear himself out. Every time he closed his eyes, Michael saw Stephan's face, sometimes nervous, like he was in the restaurant, sometimes laughing and smiling like during their time in Bruges, and sometimes the way Michael's imagination pictured him, naked, writhing under his hands. Those images in particular did nothing to bolster his resolve to keep his hands off Stephan. Eventually, he gave up and sat at the table, booting up his PC and trying to work, but he couldn't concentrate on that, either. "What is wrong with me?" Closing the laptop, he climbed back in bed, lying on his back in the dark room, staring at the ceiling. He must have drifted off to sleep because the next thing he heard was the television, which acted as an alarm, turning on.

Rolling over with a sense of relief that the night was finally over, Michael closed his eyes as the light from the television flickered in the room. His morning wood reminded him that it had been awhile, and he ground his hips into the mattress, the crisp sheets feeling really good on his dick. The announcer on the morning BBC news mentioned the time, and for a second Michael relaxed into his fantasy, until his mind caught up, and he realized they were an hour behind and he had fifteen minutes until Stephan was set to arrive. Pushing back the covers, Michael hurried to the bathroom. Taking a quick bath, he shaved, brushed his teeth, and dressed in record time. Remembering at the last second to grab some warmer clothes, he left his room just in time to meet Stephan in the lobby.

Arriving outside the desk, Michael looked around, but didn't see Stephan. Sitting down to wait, he continued watching the stairs from the lower entrance. Michael began to fidget when Stephan didn't appear, and he began to wonder if their conversation last night had embarrassed Stephan enough that he wasn't going to show. Checking his watch again, Michael got up and figured he might as well get some breakfast.

"Sorry," he heard from behind him. Michael turned and saw Stephan hurrying across the lobby. "There was an accident in one of the traffic circles, and I had to wait until I could get around." Stephan smiled, and Michael's frustration melted away. "Did you want to eat here?"

"Not really," Michael answered. He'd eaten most of his meals in the hotel all week, and he was getting a little sick of the food.

"Then we can go. I promise you interesting food and fun once we get to the beach." Stephan looked excited, and Michael let himself get caught up in it.

"I take it you're feeling better," Michael commented as they both headed toward the stairs to the vestibule.

"I am. Talking about things helped." Stephan smiled at him, and Michael felt his insides clench and throb with lustful desire. He'd spent most of the night with images of Stephan running through his head, and Michael knew in that instant that today was going to be an exercise in control, especially if all it took was a smile from Stephan to get him going.

"I'm glad," Michael said, slowing down so he could adjust things without Stephan seeing. Catching up once everything was comfortable again, Michael followed Stephan to his car.

"The ride will take about an hour, but there's plenty to see," Stephan explained as they slid into their seats, and he started the car, pulling out of the parking lot and getting right onto the freeway next to the hotel. They passed through Utrecht and changed freeways, following the signs to Den Haag, which Stephan explained was The Hague. More green fields passed outside, and Michael saw windmills, although they were the modern kind as opposed to the historic type.

After passing through a small city, they switched highways again and headed toward the beach. The name of the place wasn't pronounceable to Michael, but that didn't matter; he just continued looking out the window. "Over there," Stephan said, taking one hand off the wheel as he pointed, "those are acres of greenhouses. The ground here is very fertile, but it doesn't get warm enough, so greenhouses were built so we can grow vegetables most of the year." The sun chose that moment to peek from behind the clouds, and Michael saw the reflection of what had to be thousands of panes of glass. "See, that's how it is here. We're close to the shore, so they don't get the sun as much. It'll shine for a while and then the clouds will move in again."

The farmland quickly faded as they approached The Hague. Passing through the city, they continued on until Stephan explained that they were approaching the beach area. Stephan exited the freeway, and they drove surface streets, passing through what looked like a shopping area. Stephan pulled into a parking structure, getting in line, and they waited until they could enter and pull into a place. "It looks like we made it," Michael commented.

"Yup, and it didn't take very long, either. Sometimes, the drive can be long because of traffic," Stephan explained as they walked toward the exit of the parking structure. "It will be busy today."

"How do you know?" Michael asked, looking around as traffic passed by on the main road.

"It's sunny. Everyone will be looking to come here today," Stephan said, as they walked down the shopping street and then turned down a wide walkway. Traveling between two buildings, the walkway opened up to a wide expanse of beach. The sun shone off the water, and Michael craned his head to look first one way and then the other. A large pier with a pavilion jutted out over the water, and as they walked, Michael could see shops and restaurants built on the edge of the beach, a sort of boardwalk in front of them with the sounds of hundreds of people talking and laughing, music, and the smell of every kind of food imaginable.

"This is great," Michael said, following Stephan as they wandered. "Look," Michael said, pointing to what looked like a large sculpture.

"The whole area has sculptures depicting various Dutch tales. There's the little boy with his finger in the dyke, Hans Brinker, and a bunch more. They were all done by a famous artist." Michael heard Stephan chuckle as he nearly fell flat on his face when he half stepped off the walkway because he wasn't watching where he was going. "Would you like to get something to eat?"

Stephan led the way to a seafood restaurant, and they got a table outdoors, overlooking the entire beach. "This isn't too cold, is it?" Stephan inquired once they were seated, and Michael answered no as he peeked at the menu. The wind was cool, but the sun felt warm and the restaurant itself provided some shelter. Michael made an attempt at the menu, asking Stephan questions, and ended up ordering something completely different from what he'd expected, but it tasted good.

After lunch, he and Stephan wandered up the beach. Michael was tempted to take off his shoes and test out the water, but he reached down to feel the sand and thought better of it. They peeked into shops, and Michael stopped at one that sold every kind of kite imaginable. "I haven't flown a kite since I was a kid," Michael said with a smile before wandering on, remembering the time he and his dad had flown kites at the shore. "Can we walk out to the pavilion?"

"Sure," Stephan answered, and they headed that way. As they reached the spot where the walkway split to head out to the pavilion, Michael watched the waves break against the shore. A small round object bobbed between two waves near shore, and Michael stopped, watching. The object appeared again, and Michael took off running, tearing off his jacket and pulling off his sweatshirt, shoes left in the sand behind him. Hitting the water, he raced toward what was now plainly a small head of dark hair.

The cold shot through his legs like millions of needles were jabbing him at once. Keeping his eyes forward, he did his best to push the cold away as the water splashed against his chest, knocking the air from his lungs. Reaching his quarry, he found it was indeed a small boy, and thankfully the water wasn't too deep. Scooping him up, Michael lumbered toward the shore. Soaked pants clinging to numb legs and arms barely able to hold the boy, chest heaving and tight with cold, he stumbled out of the water and onto the sand as others gathered around. "Get some blankets," he gasped between heaving breaths as he began to shake.

Lips blue, body limp, the boy didn't stir as Michael set him on the sand and immediately began chest compressions, pushing away as much of his own discomfort as he could. "Come on, kid, breathe," he said out loud, continuing to perform CPR. The boy's head moved slightly, but Michael wasn't sure if he was doing any good until a stream of water shot out of the boy's mouth, and he began to cough. Stopping the compressions, he heard the boy continue coughing, and then he took a breath. He continued coughing and Michael helped him up. After throwing up onto the sand, the boy took a huge breath, and Michael laid him back on the sand, watching as his little chest rose and fell, the blue color dissipating from around his lips and face.

Someone arrived with a blanket, and Michael grabbed it, wrapping it tightly around the small, shivering body on the sand. Michael felt fabric against his shoulders, and he pulled the blanket around himself, shivering hard now as he felt his teeth chatter. But the best was yet to come when he saw the little boy's eyes open, looking up at him. A woman pushed her way through the ring of people, crying and fell to her knees next to the child. "He's going to be okay," Michael told her, and she looked at him, thanking him profusely as she continued crying, holding what Michael assumed was her son.

The boy began talking and crying, obviously scared. He couldn't have been more than six or seven. His mother soothed him, having him lie still, until Michael saw what appeared to be some sort of emergency services arrive. By this time, Michael was so cold he could barely function. His wet clothes clung to him, sapping away his body heat. Thankfully, the sun was still bright, but it couldn't do much against the cold of the sea water.

"Michael, we need to get you warm," Stephan said from next to him. Michael tried to get to his feet, but stumbled, falling back onto the sand.

"My legs are numb," he said, trying to get up again, but failing. More blankets arrived, and Michael felt people around him. A man in a uniform said something to him in Dutch, and Michael tried to answer, but his teeth chattered too hard, and he gave up. Thankfully, Stephan explained.

Someone tugged on his legs, and he was wrapped in more blankets as the needly feelings in his legs started again. "It's okay, Michael," Stephan said softly. "We're getting you warm." Hands stroked his legs and chest as some of the warmth began to return to his body. Looking over, he saw the little boy looking back at him, his mother still with him, talking to the people around them.

"Is he going to be okay?" Michael asked the uniformed man who was once again checking his pulse.

"Yes. We believe he will be fine," he answered in heavily accented English, and Michael sighed with relief as the shivering subsided. A gurney arrived, and the little boy was loaded onto it. Michael followed with his eyes as the mother followed behind, the small group walking along the sand. "Please tell me what happened," another man in a different uniform asked, and Michael told him what he'd seen and done. The man wrote it down. "You probably saved the boy's life," the man added with a half smile.

"I'm glad he's going to be okay," Michael said, taking a deep breath, his body feeling much closer to normal, except for the fact that he wasn't wearing pants. He realized that the reason he'd began to warm was because his wet clothes had been pulled off, but now all he was wearing were the blankets. Standing up, he made sure the blankets were wound tight around him before letting Stephan guide him off the beach and onto a bench.

"I'll be right back," Stephan told him, and he set down Michael's wet clothes, along with his shoes, jacket, and the sweatshirt he'd pulled off before going into the water. Michael pulled on the sweatshirt and jacket, leaving the blanket around his waist. At least he felt a little more normal even as people walked by, looking at him strangely. "I got you some sweat pants, and there are changing rooms just up the beach," Stephan told him before helping him to his feet.

Michael clutched the blanket, making sure he didn't flash everyone on the beach as they made their way to the changing rooms. Once inside, Michael expected Stephan to leave him alone, but he went in with him. Dropping the blanket on a bench, he took the dark blue sweatpants Stephan held out to him, pulling them onto his legs. Stephan handed him a dry pair of socks as well, and he pulled them on along with his shoes, and felt almost normal. Stephan wrung out his wet clothes, stuffing them into a plastic bag.

"Thank you," Michael said to Stephan as he stood up once again, looking to where Stephan stood, wondering about the strange look on his face. "What is it?"

"You're a hero," Stephan said softly. "What you did was the most selfless thing I've ever seen." Stephan stepped closer, his eyes locking on Michael's. Stephan stepped even closer, and Michael felt his heart pound in his chest. Michael stepped back and found his legs pressed against the bench. Stephan stepped closer yet and then stopped. "Do you not find me handsome?" Stephan asked in the otherwise-deserted changing room.

"Yes, Stephan, I do," Michael answered, and Stephan moved close enough that Michael could feel the heat from his body, and damned if his own errant libido didn't react, tenting the front of the sweatpants. "But we shouldn't do this," Michael said, doing his best to clear his mind. "You're my friend, and you're still getting over Heinrich," he said, and he saw Stephan's expression fall. "It's not that I don't like you or find you attractive, but I don't think getting together like this is a good idea for us." Michael reached out, touching Stephan on the shoulder, though he really wanted to pull the man into his arms and hug that look off his face. "I got involved with a friend once, and it ended very badly. I don't want that to happen again."

"Maybe you are right," Stephan agreed, but Michael could tell from his expression and the way his shoulders slumped that he was only going along with what Michael was saying. Disappointment and hurt rolled off him like the waves outside on the beach. "I just thought you found me attractive."

Damn, he hadn't meant to make Stephan feel bad. He just thought he needed a friend a lot more than he needed a lover, particularly someone he knew he was going to leave behind when his project was over. That wasn't fair to Stephan, but he wasn't sure how to make him understand that without hurting him. To make matters more difficult, voices outside got louder, and soon they had company. Stephan turned and walked outside. Michael grabbed his things and followed, seriously wondering if he'd just lost a friend. "Stephan," Michael said as he caught up with the other man, hoping to find a place where they could talk.

Stephan stopped and turned, waiting for him. "I understand. You aren't interested in me, and I can't change that."

"Stephan," Michael interrupted urgently, "that's not it at all." Michael stepped close. "I find you very attractive. You're probably one of the sexiest men I've ever met in my life. But you're also a friend, and the fastest way to lose a friend is to have sex with him. I also just got out of a relationship with another man, and I don't want you to be some sort of rebound guy. And you're still trying to get over Heinrich." Michael swallowed hard, looking around, thankful that the area where they were standing was nearly deserted. "My track record with guys is, like, zero, Stephan. Devon and I dated for almost six months, and that was the longest relationship I've ever had. Besides, you know I'll be going home in the fall. Is that fair to you?"

"I'm a man, not a boy. I am able to make up my own mind? Yes? If you do not find me attractive, fine. But if you do and you refuse me, then... then you're not a hero, you're a coward!" Stephan stood where he was, arms folded over his chest, staring into Michael's eyes.

Michael felt his resistance crumbling. Stephan's blazing eyes and the set of his mouth were damned attractive. The man had fire, Michael had to give him that. But the fact remained that getting involved with anyone right now was not a good idea. "How about if we take things slow?" Michael proposed, his willpower crumbling under his own desire. "We work together and we'll see each other quite a bit over the next few weeks."

"You mean like dating?" Some of the tension left Stephan's body.

"Yes. I mean exactly like dating. Okay?" Michael wasn't really sure this was a good idea. In fact, he was fairly sure it was one of the worst ideas he'd ever had, but the scowl faded from Stephan's face, replaced by the same excited smile he'd seen the day before when Stephan had shown him the Michelangelo sculpture. For one thing, he wasn't sure he could resist Stephan for very long, but this would at least give them time to think. "Can we put these wet things back in the car and then enjoy the rest of our day?"

Stephan nodded. "Okay." He led the way back to the car, and Michael placed the bag of wet clothes in the trunk. "So, does this make you my boyfriend?" Stephan asked. Michael spun around and saw the wicked grin on Stephan's face. "I am not stupid, Michael. You are stalling. I do not know why, but if this is what you want, I can go along with it." Stephan stepped very close, and Michael knew that keeping his hands off Stephan was going to be even more difficult than he thought.

# CHAPTER
## Six

MICHAEL flexed his legs in the cramped airplane seat but found himself smiling slightly nonetheless. The last two weeks had been very interesting. He and Stephan had settled into what seemed to be a very amicable friendship. Even though it was obvious to Michael that Stephan wanted more, somehow Michael had been able to resist his energetic and very handsome coworker. There had been times when he'd seriously considered throwing caution to the wind and pursuing Stephan with the same gusto he'd displayed with his past partners, but something always held him back.

"Would you like something to drink?" the flight attendant asked as she wheeled her cart down the aisle. Michael requested a diet soda, even though he really wanted a drink, and thanked her when she handed it to him before moving to the next row.

Last weekend, Stephan had taken him to Amsterdam, and they'd had fun on one of the city's canal tours. They'd also toured the Anne Frank house with its displays and hauntingly, nearly empty small spaces. Moving through the once-hidden rooms, Michael had looked in open-mouthed awe at the tiny rooms where so many people once lived in near total silence for so long. Off the main room, Michael knew immediately which room had been Anne's by the movie star photographs still attached to the walls. Coming out of the rooms and out of the house, Michael heaved a deep breath once he and Stephan were back on the street.

"Powerful, isn't it?" Stephan had asked once they were outside, and Michael had nodded, not really in the mood to talk. "Come on,"

Stephan had said, taking his hand, leading him away from the house museum and along the canal toward a bustling street filled with shoppers. "This is the Newendyke, the main shopping street." They'd walked and looked in a few shops, Michael's mood lifting with each step, and soon he'd been smiling as Stephan pointed things out to him.

They'd both chuckled at the irony of modern stores on the main floors of buildings that leaned out over the street and were probably hundreds of years old. As darkness approached, Stephan had taken Michael on a walk through the red-light district with its famous windows. They'd had a ball when the ladies had winked at them or moved provocatively as they'd walked by. But it was the large penis fountain in the middle of the district that had had them both giggling like kids, and Stephan had insisted on taking Michael's picture standing in front of it. *Now that was a souvenir you didn't get everywhere.*

Michael's project had progressed well over the past few weeks, and his tasks were on schedule, although he had serious concerns regarding the artificial time constraints that Curtis was placing on the project. Michael had squeezed almost every bit of fat out of his project schedule, and he was becoming worried that any delay or problem would cascade throughout the entire project schedule with no chance of catching up. Sipping from his soda cup, Michael set it on the tray table of the empty seat next to him and thought about pulling out his plans to go over them one more time, but he knew them by heart, he'd been over them so often, so he left them in his computer bag and instead leaned back in his chair, closing his eyes.

As had so often happened in the past few weeks, his mind settled on thoughts of Stephan. Why the other man had such an effect on him, Michael didn't know or even understand. He'd been with many guys before, and none of them had ever affected him this way. He suspected it was simply because he wasn't allowing himself to act on his attraction and kept trying to put the thoughts out of his mind, but that seldom worked.

What stayed with him most was the worried look and the nervous way Stephan had chewed on his plump lower lip when he'd said good-bye the night before, and Michael figured Stephan was getting a small taste of what would happen in the fall when Michael left the Europe office for good. Michael was only going to be back in his office for a week and then he'd return to Europe, but the trip seemed to act like a bucket of cold water for Stephan. And if Michael were honest with himself, he'd been feeling the same effect. Pulling out a book, he decided to read to pass the time and help occupy his thoughts.

A few hours later, Michael finally read the last page of his paperback, realizing he must have read almost every word twice because he simply wasn't able to concentrate very well. The closer he got, the more he realized he was going to have to deal with his boss and whatever off-the-wall notion had been planted in his head over the weekend.

An announcement that they were approaching the airport settled Michael's still-jumbled thoughts, and he made sure all his things were put away. Twenty minutes later, the huge plane landed, and Michael grabbed his carry-on and filed off with everyone else.

Winding through secured hallways, he made his way to the lower level of Dulles International, where his passport was checked, and he collected his bag for customs before having it and himself scanned again before re-entering the airport for his final flight home. A few hours of waiting and a short flight later, Michael got his bag once again and left the small airport, figuring he'd catch a cab home.

"Michael." He heard a voice carry over the sounds of people loading and unloading. "Michael." The voice got louder, and he realized it was calling to him.

Michael turned and looked. "Devon? What are you doing here?"

"I came to pick you up," he said a little breathlessly. "You'd asked me to before you left, and I figured no one else would, so I came so you wouldn't have to take a cab or anything." Devon looked tired, and Michael wondered what was wrong. Devon said nothing, however. He simply turned toward the parking structure, so Michael followed behind him, placing his bags in the trunk once they arrived at the car. Michael got in the passenger seat, letting the quiet overtake him for a few seconds.

When they exited the parking structure, Michael paid for the parking, and they rode toward home. Devon seemed quiet, which was unusual for him, and Michael wondered why for a few seconds, but he was so tired, nothing occupied his mind for long except his need for almost immediate sleep.

"I missed you, Michael," Devon said softly, and Michael rolled his head on the seat back, his eyes sliding open. "I think I was wrong to end things the way I did." Michael sighed, but said nothing. Of all the things he might have expected, this possibility hadn't been on his radar at all. "Michael, did you hear what I said?"

"Yes, I did, Dev, but I don't know what you want me to say." Michael shifted in the car seat. "When you dropped me off at the airport, you dumped me, and now, three weeks later, you pick me up again and want to get back together." Michael's mind tried to find purchase around the idea but couldn't. It seemed almost laughable, and it would have been if he thought for a second that Devon was kidding, but Michael knew he was serious. "I don't know what to tell you except I've begun to move on."

Michael heard Devon gasp, his head snapping around and the car veering toward the other lane for a second. "You already met someone else!" he accused with both his words and eyes.

"Watch the road, Dev, and no, I haven't met anyone else. Not really. I did make a friend who wants to be more, but I'm not ready yet. Besides, you dumped me, remember? Before you dropped me at the airport, if I remember correctly." Michael's anger rose quickly. "And now, when I don't feel like coming back to you when you crook your little finger my way, you get pissy." Michael stopped and swallowed, trying to keep his near exhaustion from making him say something he was going to regret.

"Sorry," Devon replied in a half whisper before lapsing into blessed silence. Michael didn't know quite what to think, to be truthful. Part of him wanted to tell Devon to take him to his place. He knew he could play Devon's slim body like a violin and that the sounds he would make would be music to Michael's ears. Devon always made the best sounds, especially when Michael held him down, depriving Devon of what he wanted. Devon would strain and stretch to get what he wanted, making the most delicious noises. And his tight body.... Michael shuddered in his seat as he thought of the way Devon reacted to his every touch, the way he felt against him and around him.

"Do you want me to take you home?" Devon asked, his question cutting through Michael's thoughts.

"Yes," Michael answered before he could change his mind. He was too tired to argue with either Devon or himself at this point. Devon took the exit near Michael's home and a few minutes later, pulled up in front. "Thank you, Devon," Michael said, before getting out of the car and lifting his bags out of the trunk.

"Do you want me to come in with you?" Devon asked, and Michael had to smile at his persistence. Michael set down his bags and walked around to where Devon waited by the driver's door. "Dev," Michael said, stroking his cheek lightly, "you need to move on. You told me weeks ago that we weren't in love, and you're probably right. You deserve to be loved. And for the record, I missed you too." Michael leaned forward, kissing Devon on the forehead. "I'll talk to you later, okay?" Devon nodded and got back into the car. Michael walked behind, picking up his bags. Devon was gone before he reached the front door.

Unlocking the door, Michael wondered if he'd made a mistake letting Devon go. In his heart he knew he'd probably done the right thing, but damn, a good, old-fashioned romp in the sheets might have been fun. Dropping his bags just inside his door, he left them behind and headed straight for the refrigerator, thankful that he'd left a few beers inside. Popping one open, he took a swig and carried it back toward the living room, where his neighbor had left his mail on the coffee table. Setting down the bottle, he went through what was there, throwing away the junk and placing the bills aside for payment. He'd paid most everything through his computer, but he needed to check that he hadn't missed anything. Finishing his beer, Michael walked to the bathroom, where he cleaned up and stepped beneath the shower. After washing away the travel and the smell of airports and plane seats, Michael climbed into his own bed for the first time in weeks. *Damn, that felt good.*

His phone began ringing, and Michael groaned and made no move to try to reach it, but the damn thing kept making noise, so he grabbed it off the nightstand and mumbled something barely coherent.

"Michael." He heard Stephan's voice and his eyes popped open.

"Yeah, it's me. I just got home," Michael said, his brain switching back on as he peeked at the time. "Isn't it pretty late there?"

"Yeah, but you said you weren't getting home until about seven there, so I wanted to make sure you made it okay." Stephan sounded tired, and Michael wondered if he'd gone to bed and set an alarm just so he could call him. Even if he hadn't, it was a nice thing for him to do. "When will you be back?"

"I get in next Sunday morning, and I'm supposed to go to my new apartment in Aud Loostrecht. At least I'll have a more permanent place to stay than a hotel."

"That's good. I will let you sleep."

"I'll call later, I promise," Michael said before hanging up the phone. It was the last thing he remembered until the sun shone through his windows the following morning.

MONDAY morning came all too quickly, and Michael got himself out of bed and into his office early. He had plenty to do, and he'd been up for hours, since his body still hadn't figured out quite what time zone he was on. "Morning, Michael," Kyle greeted him as he walked by, stopping at his door. "How's it going?"

"As well as I can expect," he answered. Things had been going amazingly well, almost too well, and Michael kept trying to figure out when the problems would start to crop up. "Our partners in Europe are doing a great job, and development seems to be on track. How are things here?"

Kyle looked around and shut the door. "Crazy. Curtis's been impossible." Kyle flopped into one of Michael's visitor chairs. "Every single issue, no matter how small, is suddenly the end of the world. And once he finds out, Curtis is in Mark's office in five seconds complaining and making a mountain out of a molehill." Kyle sighed loudly. "What surprises me is that Mark lets him. The man's a director, for Christ's sake, and he goes running to Mark over everything. What's worse, Mark believes all that crap and thinks the sun rises on Curtis's ass. I used to love this job, and now I hate coming in every morning. Managing projects is partly managing issues. They happen—we fix them and move on or adjust where we need to, but this is getting ridiculous."

"I got some of that last week," Michael started to say, careful of how much he confided, "but I just thought it was the distance. Any idea what's behind all this?"

Kyle shook his head. "No idea whatsoever, but I hope to God it stops soon, or my head is going to explode." Kyle got out of his chair and opened the door, leaving Michael's office. Wondering just what the hell was going on, Michael began opening his files and making updates before preparing the materials for his weekly meetings.

Michael spent the morning checking in with his team members and making calls to Europe. Regardless of where he was physically located, he could not let things slide. In the afternoon, he ate lunch at his desk and sent out agendas for the following day's meetings. He had just wadded up the wrapper from his sandwich when his desk phone rang, the display showing Curtis's number. He automatically tensed, wondering again why he let Curtis get to him like that. Pushing away the nervousness, he answered the phone.

"Michael, could you come down to my office?" Curtis asked in a very rushed tone of voice. Michael was getting used to the fact that he always sounded that way, but this time he seemed even more hurried than usual. Grabbing a notebook, Michael got up from his desk and walked down the hall to Curtis's office, knocking lightly on the doorframe. Curtis was on the phone, but motioned for him to have a seat and close the door. Michael complied and waited until Curtis hung up.

"I was just on the phone with the CFO of Europe, and he's thrilled with how the project is going and the way you're keeping him in the loop," Curtis told him, looking almost as though he could hardly believe it. Michael did not understand this attitude, or what he'd ever done to Curtis to make him act this way. Michael had a solid record of successful projects. In fact, he'd successfully completed some of the biggest and most complex IT projects the company had ever done. His only consolation was that Curtis seemed to treat everyone the same way, so maybe it wasn't him. Curtis leaned back in his chair, but Michael felt his supervisor's eyes on him all the while. "I understand that you've made some friends in the office."

"I'd like to think so. Building good working relationships will make the project run smoother and help build trust should any issues arise later," Michael answered, but he wondered if Curtis was driving at something else.

"You know you have to be careful how you spend your free time," Curtis said, and Michael cocked his head slightly, wondering just where Curtis was going with this. "People have noticed who you're spending your free time with."

Michael shrugged. "So? It's my free time, and I can spend it the way I wish, not that I have much of it. I get to the office before eight, and I usually turn on the lights because I'm the first one there. And I rarely leave before six." Michael could feel himself getting defensive, but he didn't like what Curtis was insinuating. He worked hard, always had. "I take work home most nights. On the few weekends I've been there, I've taken some time to get away and see things. I haven't spent all my time playing tourist or anything, so I don't understand what the issue is." Michael let a challenging note creep into his voice. He had a firm belief that time outside the office was his and none of anyone's business. He already knew that as a new person working in the office, he'd be under scrutiny, and he'd behaved accordingly. He'd spent a lot of time with Stephan, but other than eating lunch together, their time together had been off work hours.

"I'm not questioning your dedication," Curtis responded with a much softer tone than he'd been using. "I know you work hard. That's never been an issue. If you were spending your time with a woman…."

So that was it. Michael shook his head. He'd suspected on some level that Curtis might have a problem with him because he was gay, but up till now, nothing had ever been said. "How I live my personal life is no concern of yours or the company, and I believe there are policies that explain that." Michael knew the company had a nondiscrimination policy. Besides, who was Curtis to talk? Behavior advice from a man who dated one of the analysts in the office while she was still married to someone else. He'd eventually married her, but Curtis was not one to talk to anyone about proper behavior. Michael waited to see if Curtis had anything else to say, and he watched Curtis lean forward in his chair before opening a file. Then the conversation continued, this time about work and projects.

After leaving Curtis's office, Michael went back to his own office and shut the door, seething as he mumbled under his breath. Michael had never made a secret that he was gay. He'd been open and honest for years and had been promoted long after he'd come out of the closet. "Fuck," he moaned, rubbing the back of his neck with his hand. He thought crap like this was a thing of the past. For a second, he thought about going to Mark or HR, but that wouldn't do any good. If he went to Mark, he would go to Curtis to talk to him about it, and Curtis would make his life miserable. If he went to HR, they'd go to Mark. It wasn't as though he had anything concrete to bring to them. Curtis could easily say Michael had misunderstood, and he'd still make his life miserable. Before sitting down, Michael opened his door and then got to work. He had plenty to do, but the first thing he did was document the conversation with Curtis in his personal calendar, complete with the date and time.

As he was finishing, his phone rang, and Michael answered it automatically, barely taking his eyes off the computer screen. "Michael Dougherty."

"Hi Michael, it's Stephan," his friend's voice said, ringing brightly through the phone. "I wanted to tell you that we have some proposals for the marketing and branding materials ready. Do you want me to send them to you?"

"That would be great," Michael answered, stopping what he was doing so he could give Stephan his full attention.

"How are things going? Are you used to being home again, or are you still on Europe time?" He heard amusement in Stephan's voice.

"I was up at three in the morning, thank you very much," Michael replied with mock anger, and he heard Stephan chuckle on the other end of the line. "It almost seems strange to be home after so many weeks in the hotel. I actually had to cook for myself." He heard another of Stephan's chuckles.

"It seems strange to walk by where you worked and see it empty," Stephan told him, his chuckles dying away. "I actually looked for you at lunch today before I remembered that you were gone." He and Stephan had eaten lunch together, along with the rest of the guys on the team, almost every day, but it had been Stephan who'd come by every day at lunchtime. As Michael thought about it, he sort of realized that Stephan was probably coming by to make sure Michael actually ate, because the few times Stephan had been busy, Michael had nearly missed lunch altogether.

"I know how you feel. It's almost lunchtime here, and I'll probably grab something and eat at my desk."

Stephan scoffed lightly before telling him he needed to remember to eat. "Do you need a ride from the airport on Sunday?"

"No. I parked the car in long-term parking. It was less expensive than the cab fare. The apartment people are expecting me early Sunday morning, so I'll probably go right there and then sleep for a few hours." Michael wanted to talk more, but Curtis popped his head into his office. "I'll talk to you later, and I appreciate you sending the materials." Michael switched to a very businesslike tone, hoping Stephan understood.

"Okay, I'll talk to you soon." Stephan's tone didn't change, so Michael figured he'd gotten it. They disconnected, and Curtis stepped into the office, asking a number of questions about the project before leaving again. Michael went back to work, wishing he could call Stephan back just to talk to him, but it was getting late there. Stephan was probably already on his way home, and Michael had enough to do to keep him busy for hours, so he got to it.

Michael actually remembered to stop for lunch, and spent much of the afternoon in either meetings, conference calls, or running down the status of tasks, so that by the time he was ready to go home, he was completely exhausted. Leaving the office, he stopped on his way to run through a drive-through before continuing home. Michael ate in front of the television, throwing away the trash before settling in his recliner and falling asleep. He woke a few hours later, and after shutting off the television, got cleaned up and went to bed, where he tossed and turned for a few hours before finally falling asleep.

THE rest of Michael's week was more of the same, working long days before going home to try to catch up on things before crashing in his chair in front of the television, waking up later to go to bed. To Michael's surprise, Curtis had been almost helpful, which was a bit of a shock as well as a relief. On Friday afternoon, Michael finished his last meeting and packed his things, making sure he had everything before saying good-bye to his team and Curtis before heading out a little early. His phone rang just as he was leaving the building. "Hello," Michael answered as he walked to his car.

"Were you planning to be in town all week and not call?" A deep voice resonated through the phone.

"Probably," Michael answered honestly, a smile spreading on his face.

"I know how you are when you're on a big project, so I'll forgive you just this once, but don't do it again, Mikey."

"I won't, Jake," Michael answered, still smiling as he opened his car door before placing his things in the backseat. "This week has been near hell, and I have to catch a plane back to Europe tomorrow."

"Then you can go out with Roger and me tonight," Jake said before adding, "and I won't take no for an answer. We can meet for dinner if you want, but we haven't seen you in weeks."

"I'd like that. I can't stay out late, but I'd love to see you both," Michael replied, his mood lifting by the second. He and Jake had been friends for years, and when Jake had met Roger a few years ago, that friendship had expanded to include both members of the most loving couple Michael had ever met. "Is six at Carrabbas okay? I have to go home and get packed, but I should be able to meet you there."

"Great. I'll call ahead, and we'll meet you at six. Ciao, babycakes." The call disconnected, and Michael slipped into his car and drove home. As he did, he used the hands-free feature to call his parents and let them know that he was doing well. They talked the entire drive home, with Michael disconnecting just as he pulled into his parking space. Hurrying inside, Michael got the last of his clothes out of the laundry, folding them as he packed. He worked quickly and placed his suitcases near the front door. In the morning, he'd still have some last-minute things to pack, but otherwise he was ready. Checking over his work bag one more time, he placed it next to the suitcases before leaving to meet his friends for dinner.

He arrived at the restaurant a little before six and found Jake and Roger sitting at the bar, a martini in front of each of them. Jake saw him first, the barrel of a man hurrying forward, hugging him tightly before lifting him off his feet. "Aren't they feeding you over there?"

Michael laughed as he was hugged to within an inch of his life. "Yes, they feed me. I'm just not eating as much crap. Now put me down, you big teddy bear." Michael felt his feet touch the floor once again.

"So you're really all right?" Jake asked, stepping back slightly so he could look at him.

"I'm doing well, Jake," Michael answered with a huge smile, more than happy to see his friends. Walking to where Roger stood, Michael warmly hugged the tall, slighter man.

"We missed you, Michael," Roger told him, and Michael knew he'd hurt his friends by not keeping in touch more often. "We know you're busy, but they do have phones and e-mail over there, I believe." He knew Roger was teasing, but there was an unmistakable meaning in the light words.

"I know. I've been busy for weeks," Michael explained, taking a seat at the bar. "This project is harder than the others I've done because of the distances involved." The bartender walked over to him, and Michael ordered what Jake and Roger were having. "I haven't had much time." Realizing he was giving excuses, he said what he was feeling. "I'm sorry, I should have called."

"You bet your ass you should have, babycakes," Jake boomed, "but we forgive you. Just don't do it again." Jake winked before lifting his drink, tinking their glasses before downing the remainder of the cocktail. "So are you going to tell us what's been happening, or do we need to play twenty questions?" Jake signaled the bartender for another, and the man nodded.

Michael's head swam for a second, trying to remember all the changes from the last month. "Devon broke things off with me when he dropped me off at the airport." Both Jake and Roger made appropriate sounds of disbelief before immediately coming to his defense, like the good friends they were. "It's okay. I think we were becoming convenient for each other, although Devon did pick me up when I got back in town, and he said he wanted me back."

"Did you go for it?" Roger asked. "The kid is damned cute."

"No. Cute or not, I'm not in love with him, and he wasn't in love with me." Michael's comment seemed to surprise his friends because they both gaped at him, drinks halfway to their mouths, blinking confusedly.

Roger recovered first. "Michael, sweetheart, of course you weren't in love with him, but that never stopped you before. What gives?" Roger stared at him before looking at Jake, and Michael could almost see the two of them telepathically communicating with each other. Michael swore sometimes Jake and Roger could read each other's minds, the way they'd look at each other.

"What's his name?" Jake asked, turning from his lover to scrutinize Michael.

"Who?"

Jake shook his head before responding. "The man who has finally captured your heart, babycakes. Who else?" Jake continued scrutinizing him to the point that Michael felt himself squirm on the stool. "Puh-leeease," Jake said dramatically. "You've never mentioned the word love in relation to any of the guys you've dated. So what's his name?"

"I'm not in love with anyone. I have a friend in the Netherlands who I think would very much like to be more, but I'm not in love with him." Michael lifted his drink to shield himself from the looks he was getting from both of them.

The hostess walked to where they were seated, telling them that their table was ready, and Michael breathed a small sigh of relief at the interruption, but he knew the inquisition had just been put off. Both Jake and Roger were head over heels in love with each other, and they wanted the same thing for everyone they knew. Reaching the table, Michael sat across from Jake and Roger in what felt like the hot seat.

"So tell me about this Dutch boy?" Jake prodded as soon as the hostess had left. "Is he cute?"

"Stephan is a coworker. He works in the marketing department," Michael answered, trying to figure out how he was going to change the subject, but Jake was like a dog with a bone when it came to things like this. "He showed me around when I first got there and took me places. We went to the beach and to Bruges with some of his friends." Michael saw both of them waiting. "And yes, Stephan is attractive."

"He sounds really nice," Roger said.

"He is. Stephan showed me around Amsterdam, and we've gone out to dinner and stuff."

"It sounds like you're dating," Roger commented as he picked up a menu.

"Stephan has let it be known that he's interested in more," Michael commented, looking at his friends.

Jake placed his arms on the table, leaning forward a little. "And you're not interested?" Michael didn't answer, and he saw a small smile on Jake's face. "If you ask me, I'd say you're a little too interested."

"And what gives you that idea, oh Great Gay Oracle?" Michael retorted.

Jake and Roger shared a look, and it was Roger who answered. "Michael, you're a sweet man, but when was the last time you turned down an attractive man who was interested in you? Before you answer, I can tell you—you haven't. But you have this time, and I think it's because you could probably develop real feelings for him if you haven't already, and it scares you."

Michael didn't know what to say. Jake and Roger were hitting a little too close to home, and that worried him. "I don't think I'm really capable of loving someone." Michael bit his lip lightly at the admission.

"You know that isn't true. And I bet this Stephan has you staying up at night wondering what he's doing, and you think of him when you're alone," Jake told him, and Michael found himself nodding reflexively. "You love spending time with him, and when you're not, you think about him."

"When Devon told me he wanted to get back together, my first thought was Stephan," Michael admitted, wishing he could take back the words as soon as they'd crossed his lips.

"He makes you happy, doesn't he?" Jake asked softly.

Michael nodded. "But I don't understand how this can be. I've only known him for a few weeks, and he's a coworker. I'll only be there for a few months, and when the project is over, I'll have to leave."

"The answer isn't some big mystery. You just need to examine how you feel and maybe take a chance," Jake said as he reached over to Roger, patting his lover's hand. Their server approached the table, his eyes widening as he stared at Jake and Roger's joined hands. He took their orders and left again. "Let's talk about something other than Michael's love life," Roger commented. "So tell us about all the things you've seen with your Dutch hottie." Roger winked in jest.

Michael reached into his jacket pocket. Pulling out his phone, he shifted slightly and showed them his pictures. "Is that what I think it is?" Jake said with a laugh as a view of the penis fountain flashed in the screen.

"Yes. That's in the red-light district," Michael explained before going on to the next picture.

"Is that Stephan?" Roger asked, and Michael took the phone to look at the picture. It was one that Hans had taken of the two of them while they were in Bruges. Michael nodded, handing back the phone. They continued flipping through the pictures, stopping at one point and looking at each other again.

"What?"

Roger handed him the phone, and Michel found himself looking at a picture of Stephan, shirtless, lying on what appeared to be the bed in his hotel room. The smoldering look on his friend's face momentarily stopped Michael's breath as he stared at the image. Roger reached for the phone, and Michael instinctively pulled it out of his reach. Stephan had meant this picture for him, and Michael didn't feel like sharing it.

Changing the camera to the next picture, he swallowed when he saw Stephan wearing nothing but a pair of briefs, lying on what had been his hotel room bed, arms curled around his pillow, eyes looking sultrily up at the camera. Changing the picture again, the phone returned to pictures he'd taken. Handing back the phone, Michael wondered just how Stephan had taken those pictures. They must have been taken when he and Stephan had had dinner a few days before he'd left, and Michael had been called to the desk, leaving Stephan alone in his room.

"Well, I'd say that answers that question," Jake said as he continued looking at the pictures. After a few minutes, he handed back the phone. "What's with the pictures on the sand? They don't look like your normal beach pictures." Michael told them about saving the child from the water.

"So you're a hero," Roger said.

Michael shook his head. "No, I'm not. I just happened to see the kid and pull him out of the water." Stephan had made a huge deal over that incident almost up until he'd left, but Michael felt he hadn't done anything anyone else wouldn't have done if they'd seen the boy first. "I happened to be in the right place to help. That's all." From the looks on his companions' faces, they didn't seem to be buying his explanation, but they didn't argue with him.

The server brought their salads, and they began to eat, the conversation switching to Michael's plans for the next few weeks and when he would be back in town. They made dinner plans for the week he planned to be back in town as well as talked about mutual friends. The salad plates were taken and replaced by dinner plates. Jake and Roger traded bites of their dishes and laughed at small things that only the two of them understood. It wasn't that they excluded him; it was just that the two of them were so in tune with one another that sometimes words weren't necessary.

Finishing their dinners, they sat and talked over coffee for a while before paying their bill and getting up to leave the restaurant. Outside, in the warm, late spring night, they hugged and said their good-nights. "You promise you'll call us this time," Jake scolded, hugging him so tightly Michael could barely breathe. "You know we love you too," Jake added releasing him from the hug.

"I will, I promise," Michael said, getting a hug from Roger. "I'll call you late in the week." Michael nodded his head for emphasis. He'd missed his friends when he'd been away, he really had, and he felt guilty for ignoring them.

"You better," Roger scolded, "and you have to let us know how things are going with Stephan." Michael wasn't sure he was going to allow things to go anywhere, but those pictures on his phone had sure gotten him thinking, which was Stephan's intention, of that Michael had little doubt. *The little minx.*

"I'll call you, and we'll get together in a month," Michael said, as they parted, and he headed for his car. Driving home, he couldn't get those pictures out of his mind.

Once home, Michael made sure he had everything packed and as ready as he could. Taking his phone to his personal laptop, he downloaded the pictures and couldn't help himself from clicking on the pictures of Stephan. They displayed full-size on his screen, and Michael stared open-mouthed at the sensual photographs. They weren't professional, by any means, but that didn't matter at all.

Stephan's skin glistened in the light, his slightly olive tones accentuated by the white of the duvet, and the way he seemed to be looking right at him kept Michael from looking away from the photographs. Eventually, he shut down the laptop, packing it back in his work bag. Turning on the television, he reclined in his chair, watching whatever was on until he felt himself starting to fall asleep. Getting up, he turned everything off before getting ready for bed. He almost reached for his phone to take another look at the pictures of Stephan, but resisted. Cleaning up, he climbed into his bed, hoping he could sleep, but knowing he'd be seeing Stephan in his dreams, whether he wanted to or not.

# CHAPTER
## Seven

THE flight to Amsterdam seemed even longer this time for some reason, probably because the battery on Michael's laptop gave out barely an hour into the flight, and the book he was reading turned out to be a complete dud. The in-flight magazine was about as interesting as a root canal, so Michael tried to sleep and ended up watching movies and waiting for the time to pass.

When the flight attendants served breakfast and then got the cabin ready for landing, Michael was so ready to be back on the ground he could barely sit still. Finally, the plane landed, and they taxied to the terminal. This trip, he knew what to expect, and easily passed through passport control and customs before heading to where he'd parked his car. Michael loaded his things into the trunk, taking out the printout of the directions to the apartment the woman he'd talked to on the phone had sent to him. After paying for his parking, Michael drove out of the airport and got onto the freeway.

The directions seemed rather simple, but that proved to be deceptive, especially after he got off the freeway, but he found the building eventually. The apartment building was located on a small strip of land between two lakes, and as he pulled into the small front circular driveway, the sun rose just high enough to shine on the sparkling water. Getting out, he couldn't stop himself from walking to the street to gaze across at the water with the buildings of a small town rising in the distance. "It's beautiful isn't it?" a voice asked from behind him. Starting slightly, Michael jumped and turned to see a tall, impressive woman standing just behind him. "I did not mean to startle you. I'm Marta, and are you Mr. Dougherty?"

"Yes," Michael answered, smiling at her. "I appreciate you being here so early on a Sunday morning." He shook her offered hand and followed her into the building, where she motioned him inside a small office.

"I got the signed contract from your company last week," she said as she sat behind a small, immaculate glass desk. "I just need you to sign the rules, and I can give you the keys." She handed him a paper in English, which Michael signed, and then she gave him a copy. "I had planned to put you in number fourteen, but a unit opened up on the other side of the building, and I thought you would like that one better. It has the same floor plan, except that the deck outside adjoins the dock, and you can walk directly out beside the water."

"That would be wonderful," Michael responded with a smile. He hadn't thought he'd have a water view.

She handed him his keys and a garage door opener before getting up, and Michael followed her. "Here's your mailbox. The small key on the ring opens it, and the key ring itself activates the sensor to open the main doors." She demonstrated and led him through to the hallway. "You have apartment eight." She led him to the door, and Michael opened it, following her inside. "The rooms are air-conditioned, but please turn it off when you leave. There's a unit in the living area and the bedroom." She took him through the apartment, showing him the living area, bedroom, and bathroom, which was huge with built-in drawers, a closet, and cubicles for clothes, as well as all the other things he could need.

Afterward, she led him back out into the main portion of the apartment and opened a door to another bathroom and finally what looked like a closet. "Here's the laundry area. When the time comes, I will be happy to show you how to use it. It is very different from what you have in the US. Some of our clients have a hard time using them, so I show them so they know what to expect. The sheets will be changed and the apartment cleaned once a week. Yours is done on Tuesday. I know you will be at work, but if you need anything special, leave a note and we will help any way we can. In case of an emergency, we live upstairs in unit twenty. There is someone in the office Monday through Saturday during the day."

"I would never bother you unless it was an emergency," Michael assured her, and she asked if there were any other questions.

"Oh, I need to show you where to park." She led him out of the apartment and back out front. "Is it okay if I ride with you? I can show you easier that way." Michael nodded and unlocked the doors. He climbed into the car and she did too. "Pull out and make a right and then another." Michael did as requested, turning the corner. "Turn into the drive right there," she instructed. Michael did, and they pulled up to a small control box. "The opener will raise the door." She pressed it, and the door at the bottom of the ramp opened. Michael eased forward and pulled in under the building. She directed him to a space. "This one is yours," she said, and Michael parked. They both got out, and she led him through a door in the back of the garage and up a circular staircase to the main floor.

"Thank you," Michael told her.

"You are very welcome. If you need anything, please let me know. I will be around today, but normally on Sundays we are away." She walked down the hall and climbed the far stairs while Michael went back down to his car. It took him three trips to bring his luggage up and into the apartment. He figured he should put his things away, but he was tired, and the bed looked good. Closing the curtains, he slipped off his shoes before lying on the bed. The bedding seemed to curl around him. Everything felt so soft and comfortable that soon Michael drifted off to sleep, reminding himself that he shouldn't sleep too late or he'd throw his body more out of whack.

The oddest sound drifted into Michael's sleeping brain. He knew he was asleep, or half asleep, anyway. Comfortable and warm, he had no intention of getting up, but that sound came again. Curious what it could be, Michael cracked his eyes open. Feeling woozy and slightly disoriented, he got off the bed and walked through the apartment, nearly tripping over one of his suitcases. Swearing at the damned thing, he walked to the front door, cracking it, but saw nothing. The noise came again, and this time from close enough to his ear that he jumped before he realized it was the buzzer for the outside door. Grumbling, he grabbed his keys from the table and walked bleary-eyed toward the front to see who was playing jokes on him.

At the glass doors, he saw no one and was about to turn around. Looking into the lobby, he saw what appeared to be a familiar figure walking toward the front doors. Pulling open the glass doors, he walked into the lobby. "Stephan," he called questioningly, not really sure it was him. The man turned and smiled before walking toward him. "What are you doing here?"

Stephan stopped. "You told me you were getting in today, and I thought you would need something to eat. I should not have come," Stephan added, the disappointed look on his face tugging at Michael's heart.

"No, it's not that. I'm just surprised to see you." Michael checked his watch. It was after noon, and he'd been asleep for a while. "Come back to the apartment if you like," Michael added with a yawn. "I'm sorry, I just woke up." Michael yawned again, covering his mouth as he waited for Stephan to approach. Holding the door open, he waited for Stephan to enter before leading the way to his apartment.

Michael unlocked the door, but Stephan stopped in the hallway. "I should not have come. You were asleep, and I should not barge in on you. It was rude and I should go."

"Stephan," Michael started to say, stifling another yawn. "I'm glad you're here," he said truthfully, finally beginning to wake up. Holding the door open, he waited for Stephan to enter before closing it behind them. "I was surprised to see you, but I'm not unhappy about it at all."

"I should have waited to see you tomorrow at work, but I...." Stephan wandered to the sliding doors that led to the deck. "I missed you, Michael," Stephan added without turning around. "I know I have no real right to, but the week you were gone was quiet and lonely."

Michael wasn't sure if he should go with the instincts that were building inside, so he tried to change the subject. "How did you know which apartment I was in? I didn't know until I arrived a few hours ago."

"I knew this is where they put up people relocating from the States, and your name is already on the mailbox." Stephan kept talking to the glass doors, and Michael stepped toward him, placing a hand on his shoulder, but Stephan did not turn around. "I know I'm being a fool. You've said before that you weren't ready and...." Stephan heaved a huge breath and sighed. "I missed you and wanted to see you. I let that cloud things." Stephan stepped away, and Michael felt his hand slip from Stephan's shoulder and back to his side.

"Stephan," Michael called quietly, stepping closer, his heart racing in his chest. Placing his hand on Stephan's shoulder to turn him, he saw Stephan's big eyes, full of doubt. "I'm really glad you're here." Stephan turned fully, and Michael got closer still. Stephan's eyes locked on to his, mouth parting slightly. Michael knew what Stephan was hoping for, and Michael warred with himself up until the split second before he touched his lips to Stephan's.

The guns went immediately silent, the war over instantly, and he knew he'd both capitulated and won at the same time. Michael had been trying to keep Stephan at a distance for one reason or another for weeks, and as soon as their lips touched, at the first taste of the other man's mouth, he knew just what a fool he'd been. An added bonus was the almost immediate surrender to him he felt from Stephan's body. The other man leaned against him, holding on to him as he pressed his body to his, Stephan parting his lips, letting Michael take what he wanted from the beautiful man. Michael's fingers slid through Stephan's long, silky hair as he deepened the kiss, Stephan making these small needy sounds that sounded as musical and grand as any symphony. Michael devoured Stephan's mouth, his body aching as he held the smaller man close, Stephan's head cupped in his hand. Then, gradually, he softened the kiss, Stephan's sweet lips lightly touching his before the connection broke. Michael opened his eyes and saw Stephan's shining back at him, a smile on his red lips.

Stephan didn't move, and Michael blinked a few times until he realized Stephan was waiting for him. Stepping back, he looked at the other man for a second before kissing him again, this time pulling him into a tight embrace, mashing their bodies together. Michael's jeans became uncomfortably tight, and he felt Stephan's own arousal pressing against his hip.

Michael's head swam as he lost himself in the kiss. Stephan's lips, the heat from his body, and the way his silky hair felt between his fingers, all combined to drive Michael's senses wild. At that moment, all control or conscious thought left him, and instinct began to take over. Soft mewling sounds from deep in Stephan's throat accompanied the kisses, letting Michael know just how much Stephan wanted what Michael could give. No, something flashed through Michael's mind, something nebulous, but Michael knew instantly that Stephan didn't just want Michael's touch, he also *needed* his touch, and that realization had Michael's mind floating on air. Finally, he released Stephan from the kiss, pulling away so he could look at the man in his arms. Stephan's swollen lips, red and full, silently begged for more while Stephan's eyes met him in almost a prayer asking for what he needed without, it seemed to Michael, really knowing what it was he needed.

"Stephan," Michael said breathily, "do you know what it is you're doing? What you want?"

Stephan nodded, but said nothing, and Michael waited, knowing he had to make Stephan verbalize just what it was in his heart. He had to hear it as much as Stephan had to say it. "Yes, I want you. I've wanted you for weeks, and while you were gone, I missed you like a limb. I missed seeing you and talking to you." Stephan looked away. "I know you will think I'm wrong, but I kept thinking of you, wondering…."

Michael turned Stephan's head with a finger beneath his chin, leaning down, and Stephan angled his head up so their mouths touched in a tender kiss that sent fire racing down Michael's spine. His lips slipping away, Michael waited to see what Stephan would do, but he stood where he was, looking up at him, brown eyes full of insecurity that Michael initially interpreted as doubt, but then he realized Stephan was waiting for Michael to make the first move.

Placing his hand on the small of Stephan's back, he increased the pressure slightly, and Stephan walked through the living room, letting Michael guide him with just the barest touch. In the bedroom, he pulled his hand away, and Stephan stopped, looking at him in silence. "You must talk, Stephan. I don't know what Heinrich told you, but you have to talk to me. I want to hear your voice, your sounds, I want you to tell me what you like and what you don't. I want to hear you as well as see, taste, and feel you."

"But…," Stephan stuttered.

"You must always ask for what you want. I'll decide when and if you get it, but you must never be afraid to ask, and you must always say if you do not like anything." Michael touched Stephan's chin. "Always. I don't play games and I don't fool around. If we do this, it's an expression of our feelings for one another." Michael nearly gasped as he said words he'd never told anyone else. With Devon, the things they did in bed were games. Yes, he'd cared for him, but they played together and had fun together. Their sex was just that, fun. Michael knew that the time with Stephan was going to be much more than that. His heart was already engaged in a way he hadn't felt in a very long time, if ever.

Stephan nodded, but said nothing, and Michael knitted his eyebrows together, wondering if Stephan hadn't understood. "I don't know what to ask for or say."

Michael moved closer. "What do you want?"

"I want you to touch me. I want to touch you, I want…." Stephan's voice faded to a gasp as Michael placed a hand on Stephan's chest.

"Lift your arms," Michael told him. Stephan put his arms over his head, and Michael let his hands roam over Stephan's shirt, mapping the contours of Stephan's torso. Without saying anything more, Michael tugged Stephan's shirt out of his jeans, pulling it off his body and dropping it on the floor. Stephan moved to lower his arms, and Michael glared at him momentarily, and the arms returned to their position. Michael gave him a ghost of a smile before placing his hands against Stephan's skin.

Smooth, soft, warm, Stephan's skin caressed his palms as he stroked along Stephan's chest and sides. Michael saw Stephan's head fall back and then snap up again as he let his fingers pluck a small, pert nipple. Stephan said nothing, but Michael felt him shudder beneath his hands as his fingers traced the lines that led down Stephan's hips and just above his waist. Stepping back without breaking contact, Michael sat on the edge of the bed, tugging Stephan to him.

Stephan hissed through his teeth as Michael took a nipple between his teeth, lightly biting and scraping the skin while his hands caressed their way around Stephan's back to hold him where he was. Stephan had tried to move away. Michael would train him to stay still, but not today. Michael lessened the intensity of his touch, swirling his tongue to soothe Stephan's scraped skin, and as he let his hands lift off Stephan's skin, he felt him lean forward, his body asking silently for more. "Michael," Stephan whispered.

Looking up, Michael saw Stephan's arms shaking, and he nodded, allowing Stephan to lower his arms. Sitting back, Michael looked at the beautiful creature standing in front of him. Smooth, slightly olive skin, dark hair, deep eyes, chest heaving, legs shaking ever so slightly. Reaching up, Michael placed a hand behind Stephan's head, drawing him down for a deep kiss, then pulling him close as he rolled him onto the bed. Stephan scampered into position on the duvet. Breaking the kiss, Michael laughed slightly as Stephan gazed up at him. "You really want this, don't you?" Michael asked rhetorically as his hand played lightly over the obvious bulge in Stephan's jeans. "Take off your shoes, socks, and pants," Michael instructed as he moved away slightly so he could watch.

Stephan moved quickly, and Michael touched his shoulder. Stephan seemed to immediately understand what Michael wanted and slowed down. First one shoe and then the other hit the floor, then Stephan took off his socks, and finally slid his jeans down his legs, folding them before setting them on the floor. He was about to slip off his underwear, but Michael stopped him with a touch. Pulling Stephan into a kiss, Michael pressed him back onto the mattress and then commenced his exploration of the beautiful body. "Michael," Stephan whimpered under the onslaught of the kiss. "Please touch me."

There was no way Michael could refuse Stephan's plea, even if he'd wanted to. Stephan seemed starved for the simplest touch, and Michael determined he was going to give it to him. He saw Stephan lift his hands again and then put them back onto the bed. "What is it?"

"Can I undress you?" Stephan asked, and Michael nodded, leaning back on the cushiony bedding as Stephan leapt to his knees, lifting Michael's T-shirt up his belly and chest. When Michael leaned forward, Stephan slipped the shirt off his arms. Michael saw Stephan's eyes widen as he looked at his chest, and he could see Stephan nearly touch him before stopping himself once again.

"What is it? Why do you keep stopping?"

"Heinrich never let me touch him without permission," Stephan admitted, his hands stopping as he looked into Michael's eyes.

Michael shook his head, trying to keep his anger from getting the best of him. "You aren't a slave," Michael retorted and then stopped. "Unless that's what you want?" Stephan shook his head. "I didn't think so," Michael added, pulling Stephan close. "We'll figure out what works, but until then," Michael said, touching Stephan's still puffy lips with his finger, "talk, okay?"

Stephan smiled. "Okay." Michael leaned back on the bed and felt Stephan's tentative touch on his chest quickly become bolder and more forceful. Stephan shifted on the bed as he straddled Michael's hips, grinning down as he rested his butt against Michael's straining, jeans-encased erection.

Without thinking, Michael pulled Stephan down, kissing him hard as he held him tight, their chests pressing together. Michael let his hands wander down Stephan's back before letting his fingers slip beneath the waistband of Stephan's briefs. Stephan moaned as Michael emboldened his own touch, slipping Stephan's briefs down, cupping those cheeks in his hands. Stephan wriggled against his hands, and Michael tightened his grip, massaging the small, tight globes before pushing the fabric further down Stephan's hips.

Stephan gasped when Michael rolled them on the bed, obviously not expecting the quick move. Michael stepped off the bed, shucking his jeans before tugging Stephan's underwear off his legs, getting both of them naked. The man was beautiful, his skin appearing darker and richer against the white of the bedding. Climbing back onto the bed, Michael lowered himself onto Stephan and felt the other man hold him as he pulled them into a tight hug. Stephan's skin felt so good against his, and he felt Stephan moving along him, their lengths sliding past one another. Stephan's little noises got louder as he squirmed beneath him, hips bucking slightly. Damned if the man wasn't the sexiest thing he'd ever seen, and to hear him make those soft moany whines for him was almost too much. Holding Stephan's arms still, he broke their kiss, trailing his lips down Stephan's neck and throat before sucking hard on a hard, nubby nipple. Stephan thrashed beneath him, thrusting his chest forward while his hips continued their near frantic movements.

"Slow down, pretty," Michael cooed as he shifted off Stephan, gliding his hand down his chest until his fingers encircled Stephan's erection. "Is this what you want?" he asked teasingly, giving Stephan a single stroke before stopping. The cry of frustration that Stephan gave him told Michael plenty. "Then take it," Michael said, gripping Stephan tightly, the perfectly sized cock sliding through his hand. Stephan's eyes closed, his mouth opened slightly, and his hips bucked as he moved within Michael's grip. "That's it, pretty. I want you to come for me. Show me what you look like," Michael crooned as he moved his hand to Stephan's movements. Watching Stephan's face, listening to his breathing, seeing his flushed skin glistening with a light sheen of sweat, Michael felt Stephan stiffen further in his hand before crying out and shooting ropy cream onto his stomach and Michael's hand.

Stephan's body went limp against the bedding, and Michael smiled as he released him, walking into the bathroom, which was just off the bedroom, where he grabbed a towel before quickly returning. Stephan hadn't moved, and Michael gently cleaned him up. Stephan's eyes slid open, and Michael saw his lips form a beatific smile. "What about you?" Stephan asked as Michael climbed back on the bed.

Michael knew what he really wanted. More than anything, he wanted to bury himself in Stephan's tight heat, but it was too soon for that. Instead he chose to let Stephan decide. Climbing on the bed, he knelt near Stephan and waited, watching as Stephan looked up at him. When Michael nodded, Stephan moved closer, lying on his belly, and Michael felt Stephan's hot mouth engulf him, nearly stealing his breath away. Head falling back, he tried to breathe as Stephan made love to him. Opening his eyes again, Michael feasted on the sight of Stephan all laid out on the bedding, perfect butt wriggling as he hummed around him. Stroking Stephan's back with his fingertips, he tried to control his errant body as it almost immediately slipped into overdrive. Michael was almost ashamed at how fast he was building, but he couldn't stop himself any more than he could stop the waves on the lake outside the apartment or the wind through the trees. "Stephan," he groaned between nearly clenched teeth as he tried to warn him. Stephan pulled away, and Michael felt his hand around him as he came with blinding intensity.

It took a great deal of effort to keep his body from collapsing on top of Stephan. Somehow Michael managed to keep himself upright, even though his brain had nearly ceased to function. Reaching for the towel he'd used earlier, Michael cleaned them up hastily before settling on the bedding and pulling Stephan to him, holding him tightly. Michael's hands roamed over Stephan's back as he lay quietly trying to figure out what had just happened. Not that he regretted the intimacy that he and Stephan had shared, not at all. He was simply trying to get his head around it, and found himself unable to do so. Things had changed between them, and Michael found that as he lay in this strange, temporary apartment, he felt more comfortable with Stephan than he ever had with Devon, even when they'd been together in Michael's own bed.

Michael felt Stephan make himself comfortable, head against his shoulders, long, black hair caressing Michael's skin like silk cloth. "Michael." He heard Stephan's quiet voice and felt his warm hand on his chest, rubbing slowly and gently. "Have you ever been in love?"

Michael took Stephan's hand in his while taking a deep breath. "Once, a long time ago, or at least it seems like that now." Stephan shifted slightly on the bed, and Michael felt Stephan hold him a little tighter. "But things happen when you're young and stupid."

"You were hurt?" Stephan asked, placing his hand in the center of Michael's chest.

"Yes. I was in college when I met Carter. He was a wonderful person, but rather shy and inward-looking. It also turned out that he was very troubled, but he kept that part hidden from everyone, including me. Sometimes I think that's what hurt the most, that he felt he couldn't tell me what was bothering him." Michael looked toward Stephan and saw his warm eyes looking back at him, silently communicating that he understood. "Carter and I had been roommates for almost two years and lovers for a year. I knew his parents were very religious and that he hadn't told them he was gay. I hadn't told mine, either, so I didn't think it was any big deal, but it was for Carter."

Stephan shifted, rolling onto his side, his head propped on his hand, and Michael shifted, looking at the ceiling. It seemed easier than looking at Stephan. "You loved him?"

Michael nodded on his pillow. "I thought the sun rose and set on him." Michael scoffed quietly at himself. "I should have known better. Who gets to find their life partner and soul mate at twenty-one? I suppose it could happen, but it's not realistic. Still, that's how I felt, and I let myself fall deeper and deeper each day. I'd get back from class, and we'd go to dinner. Afterwards, we'd go into the room to study. But all we ever studied was anatomy." Michael turned to Stephan, but he had a blank look on his face. Michael winked, and Stephan's mouth opened and he nodded.

"What happened? Did he find someone else?" Stephan asked, seemingly caught up in the story.

"No. I think I could have dealt with that easier. At least I'd have known what was wrong." Michael sighed again, trying to think if he really wanted to talk about this at all. "In the spring of our junior year, I'd gone to the library to get some research materials for a paper. When I got back, the door was locked. I unlocked it, but there was something blocking the door, and I couldn't move it. The room next door shared a bathroom, so I knocked on their door, but they weren't there, either." Michael could feel his heart beating faster, the same way it had that evening. He'd known something was very wrong, and he'd been desperate to get into the room. "I got one of the resident assistants to open the other door and walked through the connecting bathroom and into our room."

Michael looked to Stephan, who appeared to be enthralled with the story and concerned at the same time. Michael felt Stephan squeeze him close, but to the man's credit, he didn't say anything. "The room was completely dark, and the curtains had been pulled. I reached for the light switch and hit something with my hand. Reaching around, I turned on the lights, took one look, and I guess I passed out." Michael had been so ashamed of his actions that day he couldn't believe it. "Carter had hanged himself from one of the pipes above the false ceiling." Michael found that even after all these years, he could barely talk about it. "I came around quickly enough to see one of the other guys walk in, and I saw…." Michael squeezed his eyes closed.

Stephan said something, and Michael didn't understand a word, but the tone of his voice and the gentleness of his touch gave him the gist of it.

"I came around, and other people came in. Then the campus police showed up, and everyone was ushered out of the room. I don't remember much of what happened after that. I slept at some friends' place and grieved silently. No one knew about us, and I wasn't ready to tell anyone, so I stayed quiet. People expected me to be sad because he was my roommate and friend, and I went with that."

Michael shrugged and wanted to get away to be alone and grieve a little once again, but the time for that was long past now. "The police investigated, but determined only that he'd committed suicide. I went to the funeral a few days later, and his parents took me and some of his other friends aside to tell us that Carter had left a note. They told us a bunch of BS about why he took his life, but by then I knew the truth, and I knew they were full of shit." Michael opened his eyes, turning to Stephan, the anger he'd felt then flaring briefly now. "They told me Carter had left a note that he'd been very depressed and couldn't take the pressure of school any longer… blah, blah, blah."

"How did you know they were lying?" Stephan asked.

"Because I found a plain envelope in my desk that I hadn't noticed at first. No one did. Inside was a letter from Carter explaining that he'd told his parents he was gay, that they were cutting him off and pulling him out of school to send him to some ex-gay camp where he could be cured." Michael wiped his eyes before continuing, knowing the best thing to do was to get this over with so he wouldn't have to think about it. "In the letter, he said he loved me and that he would rather be dead than under his parents' control. So while I was gone, he pushed the dresser in front of the door, tied a rope over the ceiling pipes, and jumped."

Michael closed his eyes again, wondering why he'd told Stephan this at all. "That was all a long time ago," Michael added, trying to get some control of his emotions. "I'm sorry you had to listen to all that," Michael added hastily, feeling a bit like a crybaby. All that had happened years ago, and he didn't think it should still affect him the way it did. He didn't like showing weakness like that, either. "Have you been in love?" Michael asked, returning to the original question while trying to change the subject away from him at the same time.

Stephan shifted closer to him, and Michael used his weight and strength to tug Stephan on top of him, his hands stroking the smaller man's backside. "Yes. I seem to fall in love too easy."

"Did you love Heinrich?" Michael asked warily.

"I did, I guess." Stephan shook his head. "I always fall for the wrong men. I like men who are strong and forceful, and what I get are bullies. I should not be surprised, but it happens every time."

Michael growled, his hands gripping Stephan's butt as he held him closer. "I am strong and I can be forceful, but I'm not a bully." Michael captured Stephan's lips, kissing him hard to accentuate his point. Gentling the kiss, Michael tugged Stephan's lower lip with his before releasing it.

"I know you are not a bully. You are a hero," Stephan said with a smile as he wriggled his hips against Michael's. "You did not think of yourself when you helped that boy at the beach. No bully would ever have done what you did."

Michael could feel his body responding to Stephan's closeness. Stephan's body was as well. But a deep rumbling from his stomach joined by one from Stephan's had them both laughing, particularly since their stomachs actually seemed to be having a competition. "I guess they're saying food before sex," Michael commented, and his stomach seemed to agree, even louder this time. They both laughed, and Michael got off the bed before pulling on his clothes, watching as Stephan's skin disappeared beneath his own clothes, and he wanted to pull him back onto the bed right now and strip them off him again. But the man deserved to eat, and they needed to talk.

"What's that look?" Stephan asked as he buttoned his jeans.

"Nothing. I've wanted to know what you'd look like naked for weeks. I've imagined it plenty of times," Michael said as he pulled on his shirt before stepping closer. "I thought I had a good imagination, but it paled when compared to the real thing." Michael saw Stephan color slightly and look away.

"You don't have to say those things."

Michael touched Stephan's chin. "I never say what I don't mean." Michael kissed Stephan's lips tenderly. "And whoever told you that you weren't a very handsome, attractive, and totally sexy man was lying through their teeth." Michael touched his lips to Stephan's one more time. He didn't need to know who had made Stephan feel that way. It was written on his face. "I'm going to kill this Heinrich if I ever see him," Michael added, a touch of growl to his voice, then he winked at Stephan as he sat on the edge of the bed to put on his shoes. "Umm, I have no idea what's open for lunch around here."

Stephan stood up from tying his shoes. "Not much. I think there's a snack bar down the street and that's about all."

"Can we walk?"

"Certainly. But you have to watch out for the bicycles. Even out here, they'll knock you out of the way." Stephan was grinning, but Michael was certain he wasn't kidding. Those Dutch bicyclists were aggressive. Grabbing his keys and a jacket, Michael followed Stephan outside, and they walked toward what looked like a small business area down the street.

The snack bar was indeed the only business open, and they went inside, placing their orders before sitting at a table to wait. Michael and Stephan talked and talked. The food arrived, and they talked some more, laughing and sharing stories. It seemed that now that Michael had shared the worst story of his life, the rest was easy, and he told Stephan about his parents and the rest of his family, and Stephan told him about his family. "I think I told you that they live in the north. They were farmers, and my father sold the farm a few years ago and built a house in town."

"Do you have any brothers or sisters?" Michael asked as he ate a French fry.

"Two sisters, actually. They're younger than I am and still live at home." Stephan finished his lunch and threw away his trash, picking up Michael's too. They left the restaurant and walked around, enjoying the sunshine, and Stephan flashed a smile that threatened to put the sun to shame when Michael took his hand. "Where are we going?" Stephan asked after they'd been walking for a while.

Michael turned to him with a laugh. "I have no idea. I thought you were leading." They turned around and walked along the water back to Michael's apartment building. Michael expected Stephan to leave, but instead he followed him inside, and they watched television for part of the afternoon. Actually, a better description would be that they ignored the television and had fun on the sofa. In the evening, they found a small restaurant for dinner and talked. After dinner, Stephan said it was time for him to leave, and when they walked back to his car, they continued talking and kissing for an hour until Stephan actually got in the car. Michael stood out front, watching Stephan's taillights disappear before going back inside.

He spent the next hour unpacking and thinking of Stephan before cleaning up and collapsing into bed. Thankfully, tomorrow was Independence Day back home, so he'd have a full day of quiet before the phone calls started on Tuesday. Michael figured he was going to need it, but right now he was happy. Whatever happened with the project, he'd take things one day at a time. Stephan was worth it, and he'd deal with going home permanently when the time came. He still had months before then, and Michael determined, as he climbed into the heavenly bed, that he was going to enjoy them and do his best to make sure Stephan did, as well. Turning out the light, Michael cracked a window open, listening to the sounds of the night. Even though he wasn't ready to admit it to himself, and the thought of getting hurt scared him to death, deep down, Michael knew he'd begun falling in love.

# CHAPTER
## *Eight*

THE next week and a half was remarkably quiet. His project meetings went well, showing excellent progress. The European accountants had come up with some issues, and Michael had worked with them to make sure they'd get the information they would need from the system to do their work, and they'd gone back to their offices with smiles on their faces. They'd also identified two additional requirements that would require reports to be built. Michael worked with store operations to design the reports and sent the completed user requirements to the development staff back in the States, sending Curtis a copy along with an explanation. Things like this came up all the time in projects, especially once the user community really started to think about the ramifications of the project and how it would affect their daily work. Michael always tried to get them involved early, but it always took time for them to really think of all the possibilities. He kept expecting a phone call or some response from Curtis for most of the week, but nothing came. It was the kind of thing that Curtis always seemed to pounce on as a source of criticism, but all Michael got was quiet. Granted, he wasn't going to complain, not in the least—especially since on top of work going well, Stephan's and his tentative explorations were proving quite exciting.

Wednesday, however, was a completely different matter. All had remained quiet, and Michael's project continued progressing well as he collected updates from the various teams in preparation for the weekly project meeting. But about three in the afternoon, he received a phone call from Curtis bombarding him with questions. What surprised him was that Curtis seemed conciliatory. "I know the warehouse consolidation wasn't your project, but would you take a look at the documentation and let me know what you think? I understand it's going to be audited, and I'd like a second set of eyes on it before the auditors get their hands on it. Don't change anything, but let me know what you find."

"Sure. I'll look at it tonight," Michael answered, without thinking much of it. Curtis was being nice, and Michael hoped by doing him a favor, he could get on Curtis's good side. That is, if one actually existed—the jury was still out on that.

Curtis became quiet, and Michael heard the door close and the phone shift off speaker. "Could you look at it right away and get back to me in an hour or so? It's kind of important."

"Okay, but it takes more time than that to really dig into the documentation. I'll see what I can find." Michael wondered just what was going on, but this wasn't his project, so at least he wasn't on the firing line, and he'd do what he could to help if there was an issue. "Let me get started, and I'll call you in an hour with anything I can find." Michael hung up and logged into the project repository. Finding the project in question, he began printing out the information so he could read it and take notes. There was a lot of it, and Michael realized this was going to take a whole lot longer than an hour.

"How is it going?" Michael heard from the doorway. He didn't have to look up to know it was Stephan. His body knew it, too, responding immediately to the other voice. They had been careful in the office, but it was hard to make his dick understand, especially after last night.

"Really busy," Michael responded, giving Stephan a smile as he sent more documents to the printer. "Curtis wants me to review some project documentation for him, and he needs it right away."

"Is there anything I can do to help?" Stephan asked as he stepped into the office.

"Sure, but don't you have your own work to do?"

"I'm caught up for the afternoon, so I can give you a few hours." Stephan smiled at him, and Michael wondered just how he would be able to concentrate with Stephan right next to him. But there was way more work than one person could do.

"Okay." Michael got up and motioned for Stephan to sit down. Once he did, Michael stood behind him. "See this list of files labeled 'Program Specifications'? Each of these must have a corresponding unit test plan. I'll print out a view of all the specs, and you can help by matching up the test plans."

"Do I need to print them?" Stephan asked as he looked up from the screen, and Michael had a nearly overwhelming urge to close the door and…. He nearly groaned out loud when Stephan looked him up and down mischievously.

"No," Michael answered, returning his mind to the task at hand. "Just make sure one exists. That's all we'll have time for right now. The auditors will have to determine if the quality is up to standard, and that alone could take hours." Michael printed the view before navigating to the test plans. "Simply open each file and match up the program names to the specifications. I'll be right back." Michael hurried out of the office to the printer, passing by some of the guys, who waved. Michael returned their silent greetings, but didn't stop to talk. There was way too much to do. Grabbing the stack of papers, he hurried back, handing the list to Stephan while he settled on the other side of the table with the other documents and began reading. Michael knew which areas on the forms were truly important and which were fluff. He'd done projects long enough to be able to zero in on what was important: deliverables promised, requirements to meet those deliverables, risks, their mitigation, or in this case, lack of it.

"Did you find something?" Stephan asked, looking up from the screen.

"Possibly. The team identified a lot of risks both to the project and the company, but it doesn't look like any of them were analyzed." Michael made a note to check further once Stephan was done. He then moved to the deliverables and their corresponding requirements. That looked good, but when he tried to link the requirements to the testing, things fell apart again. "Damn it!" Michael swore under his breath. They hadn't linked the test cases to the requirements, and he didn't know enough to link them by content. They had done plenty of testing, but was it the right testing? Was everything tested? He had no way of knowing. Pulling out a notebook, Michael began making handwritten notes regarding what he was and wasn't seeing.

"I think I'm done," Stephan told him, walking away from the computer and over to where Michael was seated. "These specifications don't appear to have test plans." Stephan handed him the sheet, and nearly a quarter of the specs weren't checked off.

"This isn't good," Michael commented, and then he had a thought. Going to his computer, he sat down and brought up the author of the documents and the project manager. His eyes widened, and he looked again to make sure he was correct. "Why would Curtis ask me to look into one of his old projects?" Something was going on, but Michael had no idea what. Thinking, he stared at the wall, his eyes unfocused as he tried to concentrate. This project had been completed last year, so it wasn't in scope for auditing. Checking his PC, he logged on to his e-mail to see if he could catch on to anything, but there was nothing out of the ordinary. Michael thought of asking Curtis, but Curtis had already handed him a line of bull once. Picking up the phone, he dialed Kyle's number, but only got voice mail.

"Is something wrong?" Stephan asked from where he stood.

"I'm not sure," Michael answered, deciding to simply play dumb and provide Curtis with the information he'd requested. Just to be sure, Michael highlighted the files from the project, copying them to a separate space on the server. His phone rang, and Michael saw Curtis's number on the display. Michael answered it and provided him with the information he'd found. Curtis did not sound pleased, but accepted the information and hung up.

"I should make sure nothing fell apart while I was away," Stephan told him, walking toward the door and then stopping. "I forgot what I originally came for. The company is having their picnic on Saturday, and I was wondering if you'd like to go. They sent out a note last week, and I figured they might have missed you on the note."

"That would be great. Where are they holding it?"

"At Efteling. It's sort of an elf-themed place, something like Disneyland. I'll forward you the note once I get to my desk. That way you can notify HR so you'll have a ticket." Stephan flashed a grin before leaving the office, and Michael stared after him for a few minutes before returning to his work.

The sound of a throat clearing caught Michael's attention, and he looked up from his screen. "Are you getting settled back in?" Greg said as he walked in and sat down.

"Yeah," Michael answered. "How is everything here? No big issues while I was gone?"

"No, it's been pretty quiet, and accounting seems to be happy with the information you provided." He leaned back in the chair and closed the door. "Is something going on? I called back to your office to speak with Curtis, and he seemed rather frantic and said he'd call me later." That was interesting. Curtis was a director, but Greg was a vice president and technically outranked him. It was strange for Curtis to blow him off like that.

"I have no idea," Michael answered truthfully. It felt as though something wasn't quite right, but no one was talking to him, either. "It could be nothing." He didn't add that it could just be Curtis being the twit that he was.

Greg nodded, but didn't look convinced. "I have an executive-update meeting tomorrow, and I'd like to give an update on your project."

"No problem." Michael was typing as he answered. "I have a progress overview document all set." Michael pressed the e-mail send button. "It'll be waiting when you get back to your office. If you need anything else, let me know." They continued talking about the project for the next hour, and by the time Greg left, Michael felt confident that his primary project backer was on board with the project timeframe and understood exactly what would and would not be delivered, again. As Greg walked out of his office, Michael was ready to go home. He checked his e-mail one last time, found the forwarded e-mail from

Stephan, and called HR for the picnic arrangements before packing up to leave the office, very happy this day was over.

The drive from the office to his apartment took a while because the freeway took him around Utrecht and he had to deal with heavy traffic. Once he got through the city, Michael increased his speed, the windows down, letting the air clear out the cobwebs from work. His phone rang through the car radio, and Michael raised the windows, turning on the fan for ventilation before answering. "This is Michael." He half expected it to be his mother. She always seemed to call when he was on his way home.

"This is Mark."

"Hey," Michael said as he approached his freeway exit. "What can I do for you?"

"We may need to bring you back," Mark told him bluntly.

"Can I ask why? The project is going very well." Michael had no idea where this was coming from, but he felt his insides churn. If they brought him back, he'd probably never see Stephan again. "The Europeans are happy, and we're actually a little ahead of schedule. If you transition this to another PM, the project will fall behind." Michael exited the freeway before finding a place he could pull off the road. He was finding it difficult to concentrate on his driving all of a sudden.

"But what about all the issues?" Mark pressed.

"What issues? We've had some items that have been identified because the users are now engaged rather than sitting on the sidelines. It's what happens. You know that. So far there hasn't been anything that we and our European counterparts couldn't handle." Michael wondered just what exactly Curtis had been telling Mark, and he figured he might as well go for broke. "If you want me to come back, I will, but it will put the project in jeopardy." The only answer he got was silence. "If you call Greg, I'm sure he'll say the same thing." Mark still didn't say anything, and Michael waited for some sort of answer.

"You aren't bullshitting me, are you?"

"Mark, when have I ever told you anything but the plain truth?" Michael asked, knowing he'd always spoken the truth when Mark had asked him anything. Even when he knew it wasn't what Mark wanted to hear.

"Yeah." Mark got quiet again. "I'll call you tomorrow after the morning meeting and let you know what's happening," Mark told him and then disconnected. Michael disconnected as well before pounding the steering wheel once in frustration. He'd worked hard to get this project on track and where it should be. Furthermore, he'd found someone he wanted to spend time with and get to know. Sure, he'd initially not really wanted this project, but all that had changed, and it was mostly due to Stephan. Checking behind him, he made sure the road was clear before pulling back into traffic and continuing his drive toward the apartment.

He barely saw or remembered the rest of the drive. Once he was in the apartment he'd just started thinking of as his, Michael felt the same loneliness he'd felt when he'd first arrived, before he'd met Stephan or anyone else. He was starting to feel welcome, and the guys even included him in their celebrations. When one of the guys had a birthday, the tradition was to bring in these sausages in pastry, with the unpronounceable Dutch name *Saucijzenbroodjes*. Michael found he loved the things, and he'd had them at least once a week when one of the guys' wives would send them in. The office here was smaller than back home, so everyone helped everyone else, just like Stephan had helped him today. What surprised Michael most was how accepting everyone was. Curtis had said something to him weeks earlier about people talking about him, but Michael now refused to believe it, at least not in the way Curtis had suggested.

Michael opened his refrigerator, pulling out a ready-made dinner he'd bought at the grocery store and popping it into the microwave, trying to remember just how to use it. Even something as simple as that was different. What surprised Michael was the fact that he didn't care about the differences. He felt accepted and he liked it here. The microwave dinged, telling him his dinner was ready, and after getting a plate, he sat at the small table eating his pasta and watching as the lake shimmered and sailboats glided quietly past. "Damn," Michael said out loud, setting down his fork. "I can tell myself whatever I want, but it's Stephan I'm really going to miss." His friend had gotten under his skin in the best way possible. The man's smiles and the way he seemed to read Michael, warmed him—sometimes he thought Stephan could read his mind.

Pushing back from the table, he left his dinner largely untouched and opened the sliding glass doors, wandering out on the deck. He needed to think. He knew Curtis had been making a big deal out of everything he saw as some sort of issue. What Michael couldn't figure out was why, or what Curtis hoped to gain from it. Michael had always figured Curtis wasn't especially comfortable around him because he was gay, but why badmouth Michael's projects? It only made Curtis look bad too. None of what was going on made any sense to him at all. But that really didn't matter. *If Mark brought him home, it could mean so many things*, Michael thought as he wandered back and forth on the dock. Michael had worked very hard for years, and if Mark brought him home, it meant that he'd lost faith in him completely. Michael knew there was no reason for it, other than Curtis's badmouthing, but Michael couldn't figure out how to convince him.

The sky darkened, and Michael felt a slight chill off the water. Going back inside, he cleaned up what was left of his dinner and decided to go to bed early. There was nothing he could do about anything right now, and it galled him. He was a man of action—give him a problem and he started to make plans to solve it. That was what he did, but this was completely out of his hands, and he hated it.

Michael wandered through the small apartment, turning out the lights, and heard his phone's muffled ringing. Searching through his bag, he found his phone and answered it.

"Michael." He heard Stephan's voice, and Michael suddenly wondered if he'd forgotten something. "I wanted to call to say good night. I know you were busy this afternoon, but I had a great time working with you. It was interesting seeing some of the things you do."

"Thanks, Stephan. Maybe I'll be able to work with you and see what you do," Michael said, not believing his own words. Mark rarely changed his mind, and Michael knew that when Mark called him, he'd already made his decision, and there was little chance of him changing it.

"What's bothering you?" Stephan asked, and for a second Michael wondered how Stephan could read him so easily. "I can tell by your voice."

Michael debated if he should say anything at all to Stephan, but he couldn't lie to him and still look at him in the morning, even if tomorrow turned out to be his last day here. "I got a call from Mark, and he said I might need to return."

"For how long?"

"I think he meant permanently," Michael answered, and the line went silent. He could hear light breathing on the other side and then, "Oh." Michael waited to see if Stephan would say anything, but he heard nothing, and when he looked, his phone read signal lost.

Michael tried redialing, but nothing would go through. Growling, Michael tossed his phone on the sofa before flopping down as well, wondering what Stephan must be thinking right about now. Michael knew Stephan thought he'd been hung up on. "Damn it," he growled, picking up the phone again, but he couldn't get a signal, which was as annoying as hell.

Jumping off the sofa, Michael grabbed his phone and keys before hurrying out of the apartment and down the hall toward the lobby. Outside, he couldn't get a signal, either, and he began walking away from the building. His phone chirped that he was entering a service area and he waited for it to connect and dialed Stephan's number. He heard a single ring and then lost the signal again. Cell service was usually spotty out near the lakes, but he hadn't had problems like this before. Turning around, he began walking back toward the building and then around the corner in the other direction, but he couldn't get service there at all. Giving up, he walked back to the building and inside, resigned to the fact that he'd have to be sure to explain things to Stephan first thing in the morning. Opening his apartment door, Michael figured he was in for a long night.

After turning off the lights, Michael went to bed, trying to get his mind around the fact that he was most likely going to leave very soon. Lying in the bed, he stared at the ceiling, closing his eyes and trying to sleep.

A buzzing from the other room startled him, and he jumped from the bed. Half asleep, Michael wondered what the hell was happening, and then his brain cleared and he could focus. Realizing it was the door buzzer, Michael pulled on a robe and hurried to the lobby, hope springing in his chest. As he approached the door, he saw Stephan standing outside. Relief swelled through him, and Michael pushed open the door. Stephan stared at him as though looking for something and then stepped forward. Without thinking, Michael reached for him, hugging him tightly as their lips met. Michael heard Stephan moan softly. Breaking the kiss, he took Stephan's hand and led him back to the apartment, closing the door behind them. "Why did you come?"

"You said you might have to go. I had to see you." Stephan looked as though his heart was going to break, and Michael knew his eyes projected the same emotion. "I finally met someone who cared for me, who was everything I could want, and he's being taken away."

"When I lost the call, I was afraid you might have thought I hung up," Michael said, and then Stephan was in his arms, and Michael was kissing him again. Holding Stephan tightly, he steered them toward the bedroom and onto the bed, their kisses continuing as they fell onto it. As soon as they were horizontal, both of them scrambled to remove the clothes of the other. This was no artful seduction or careful lovemaking. Instead, their movements became frantic, only stopping when they were chest to chest and skin to skin. And even then, Michael wouldn't let Stephan move away from him even for a second. He didn't understand the root of these feelings, at least not yet, but the thought of Stephan being away from him for a second was intolerable.

"Please, Michael, I want you," Stephan gasped between kisses.

"You have me."

"No," Stephan said as he took Michael's hand, placing it on his hip. "I *want* you, Michael."

Michael knew exactly what Stephan was asking for, and frankly he wanted nothing more than to bury himself in the hot, tight body that was currently wriggling under him. Michael shifted slightly, and Stephan wrapped his legs around his waist, strong thighs holding on to him. "Why me, Stephan? Why do you want me?"

"Because you're strong and gentle," Stephan answered, as Michael ran a hand down his thigh and over his butt, coming teasingly close to Stephan's opening, so close he heard Stephan's voice falter with what he hoped was excitement. "Because you can do that to me with a touch," Stephan added through gritted teeth, as Michael continued exploring. "And because you're special." Stephan stopped talking as Michael skimmed a finger over his opening. Back arching beneath them, Stephan moaned loudly then growled as Michael moved his hand away. No other lover had ever told him he was special. Even Carter had never said anything like that to him, let alone trembled at his slightest touch the way Stephan was doing now. "Please, Michael."

Michael reluctantly got off the bed, immediately missing the heat from Stephan's body.

"Where are you going?" Stephan asked as he moved across the bed, his hand taking Michael's.

"I need to get some things, and I don't want to hurt you," Michael whispered as he leaned over the bed, kissing Stephan lightly before walking to the bathroom. Michael fumbled for a few seconds, not wanting to turn on the light. Eventually, he found what he needed and walked back into the bedroom. The smallest amount of light reflected off the water, lighting the window. All Michael could see was the outline of Stephan's body on the sheets, but it was enough to reignite his desire in an instant.

Setting the supplies on the table before climbing on the bed, Michael's hands stroked Stephan's skin, and he felt the other man gravitate toward him. Taking Stephan in his arms, he kissed him hard, deeply, naked skin pressing together, sharing their breath, their heat, and something that lit Michael's heart on fire.

"I want you inside me, Michael," Stephan told him softly just before Michael felt his tongue against his skin. Reaching to the table for the slick, Michael gasped when Stephan's mouth clamped onto a nipple, and Michael wondered what had happened. The last time they were together, Stephan had been docile and ever so responsive, but now he was very nearly aggressive. Truthfully, Michael wasn't sure which he liked better.

Grabbing the bottle, he turned over, pinning Stephan to the mattress. The bottle dropped onto the sheet as he held Stephan's hands in one of his, running his tongue up Stephan's throat before trailing a line of kisses and licks along his chest to a perky nipple that practically jumped into his mouth. Stephan went wild beneath him, and Michael grinned next to his skin as his lover began making those little pleasure noises that quickly built and filled the room. Michael joined him, letting his lover know just how much pleasure Stephan was giving him. If this was the last time he got to be with Stephan, he was damned well going to make it as mind-blowing for him as possible. Finding the bottle, Michael released Stephan's hands, telling him to leave them where they were. Slicking two fingers, he touched Stephan's inner thigh, and Stephan parted his legs, lifting them so Michael could get access.

That small movement displaying near complete trust blew Michael's mind and told him more than words could possibly say. Finding that small, tight opening, Michael breached his lover with a single finger, the tight heat surrounding him, sending a shiver of excitement down his spine. Adding another finger, Michael listened for any sign of discomfort but only heard Stephan's soft breathing. Then he curled his fingers and heard a gasp and felt Stephan clench around him. "Do that again!" Michael did and heard the gasps turn to moans, and then a steady stream of Dutch from between clenched teeth.

"Are you ready for me?" Another stream of Dutch was followed by a yes. Opening a condom package, Michael rolled it onto himself before making sure he was well lubed.

Entering Stephan's body was damned near a religious experience. He'd heard people talk about the connection they'd experienced with someone special, but up until that moment, Michael thought they had all been weaving a tale for the singles. Now he knew better. Stephan's body felt like coming home, and thoughts threatened concerning how he could possibly leave, but he pushed them away. If this was all he got, he'd make it the best he possibly could. Pushing deep, Michael stilled and waited for some sign from Stephan. What he got was the tightest heat around him that Michael could ever imagine. Withdrawing slowly, Michael nearly pulled out before pressing forward, hearing Stephan groan the entire time.

Damned if Stephan didn't feel great around him, and Michael wished he could see Stephan. All he could see was his form against the white of the sheets. He thought of turning on a light, but stopped, deciding to revel in and remember the feelings rather than the sight of his lover.

"Do that again," Stephan groaned when Michael shifted slightly, and the moans increased. He used those sounds to judge just how he was affecting his lover. Reaching down, Michael wrapped his fingers around Stephan's cock, stroking him to the rhythm of his movements. He liked that Stephan's pleasure was in his hands, and he loved the way Stephan trusted him. "Michael!" Stephan cried, and he felt his lover's entire body begin to quiver. Increasing his pressure, he stroked harder and heard Stephan cry out in the darkness as his own release built deep inside.

Hip movements became ragged, and Michael clamped his eyes closed as he felt Stephan's release begin and his own tear through him. A flash lit the room, and Michael wasn't sure if that was in his brain or from someplace else, and right now he didn't care at all.

Michael could barely breathe. His eyes clamped shut as he stopped himself from collapsing like a rag doll on top of his lover. Gently pulling out of Stephan's body, he heard him gasp and then sigh softly. Sliding off the bed, Michael disposed of the condom and grabbed a cloth from the bathroom, wishing he'd remembered to get one earlier. Handing it to Stephan, Michael climbed back onto the bed, and once he heard the soft sound of the cloth hitting the floor, Michael gathered Stephan into his arms, holding him tight. There was so much he wanted to ask him. Things he expected he'd have time to ask and learn, maybe experience together, but right now, it didn't look like that was going to happen.

"Do you really think you'll have to leave?" Stephan asked him softly, his mellow voice cutting through the darkness.

"I wish I knew. Mark said he thought he'd need to bring me home, and that's Mark-speak for he'd made up his mind, so get prepared. I argued my point as best I could, but he rarely changes his mind about things like this." Michael tightened his hold on Stephan, stroking his hand down his back. He tried to make himself concentrate on the few seconds Mark had seemed to waver during their conversation, but he knew that was probably him hearing what he wanted to hear. Michael stared up at the now black ceiling, wondering just what was going to happen, feeling completely helpless and angry as he wondered what he could have done to prevent this.

"I'll miss you if you go," Stephan mumbled softly, almost like he felt he had to say it, but didn't really want Michael to hear him. But he had. Angling their faces close, Michael kissed Stephan, pouring his own fear and feelings into the kiss.

"Have you ever felt all alone in a room full of people?" Michael asked, and he felt Stephan's head nod against his skin. "That's how I feel most of the time, always on the outside looking in. I have friends, good friends, but they have their own lives, and I'm always the third wheel. Even with Devon, he had his friends and went out and had a good time on his own. Most of the time we felt separate, and I think it was my fault," Michael admitted, not quite sure why he was laying all this on Stephan, but in the dark with him in his arms, it seemed easy to talk about it. "I never felt like that with you, though. When I came here, I expected to have a lot of time to myself, feeling alone and miserable. I haven't, and that's because of you. I don't know what I expected, exactly, but it certainly wasn't one of the most loving, sweetest, and most caring people I've ever met in my life." The words were on the tip of his tongue. "If I have to leave, I want you to know that I'll miss you too, very much." And that's where they stayed. He couldn't actually say the words he knew he should, but it wasn't fair. If he left, Stephan didn't need to know that Michael loved him. It would only make things harder on both of them.

Michael blinked a few times, listening to Stephan's soft breathing. He still held him and had no plans to let Stephan go. He felt Stephan shift in his arms so he could hold him back. How long they lay like that, Michael lost track. Eventually, he heard Stephan's soft breathing and a few snores, but he still stared at the ceiling, unable to sleep and afraid to move in case Stephan let go of him. Sometime in the night, Michael turned his head, the room lit just enough that he could see the outline of Stephan's face, his eyes closed.

"Damn it," he said under his breath—he wasn't going without a fight. He liked his job and the project he was doing, and he was pretty sure he loved Stephan, and he needed to fight for what he wanted. Somehow, he needed to convince Mark that Curtis had been feeding him a line of total shit. Up till now, he'd been a team player, and the team leader had been selling him up the river. That was going to stop. Somehow he was going to make Mark see the truth. This was what he did for a living, managing projects and expectations, and he just needed to manage Mark this time. He'd make his plans in the morning. Closing his eyes, Michael felt peaceful, and he finally drifted off to sleep.

# CHAPTER
## *Nine*

STEPHAN left early since he had to stop at his apartment to clean up and change clothes. Michael missed him as soon as the door closed behind him, but he had things he needed to concentrate on, and that kept him from thinking about the possible loss too much. After showering and cleaning up, Michael gathered his things and headed down to his car, leaving the building and arriving at the office early. As he entered the IS area, Michael turned on the lights and got right to work, preparing for the day.

By the time he heard footsteps in the hall, he had his daily preparation tasks completed. Looking up, he saw Greg walk by his door. Standing up, Michael followed him down the hall to his office. "What's on your mind?" Greg asked as he set his case on the table and then sat in his chair. Michael took one of the other seats, closing the door. "Mark called me last night and said he may need to bring me back." Greg's eyes narrowed and he leaned forward. "It seems my supervisor has been making it out that the project has had a lot of issues and is in trouble somehow. I tried to set Mark straight, but I don't know how successful I was."

Greg said nothing and Michael waited. "That's total bullshit," Greg responded, his South African accent very pronounced. Michael had learned that only happened when he was really angry. "I had to practically beg to get someone over here to help us with this project. You are the exact person we need for this project, and we need you here." He saw Greg checking the time. "Fucking time difference," he swore before banging his hand on the table. "People in the States have no idea what it's like over here. Eleven countries with eleven sets of laws and eleven sets of the way things are done. They think whatever they do for the States will work here, and it doesn't. You understood that right away. You're the only one who ever has, and I'll be damned if they're taking you away because of that homophobic prick you work for."

Michael's eyes widened, and he couldn't suppress a smile. "I take it you know something I don't," Michael said, even though he'd had his suspicions.

"The guy's a real prick. I've had to work with him before, and I'd prefer not to, if you want the truth. Never understood what Mark saw in him in the first place. But yes, Curtis's a prick who has a problem with the fact that you're gay. He's never said so outright, but he didn't really try to hide it with me, either. He's not the brightest bulb on the line."

Michael started to chuckle. At least others saw what he did—that gave him some hope. "Mark is supposed to call me this afternoon."

"I'll talk to him," Greg told him as Michael got up. "And don't worry, I won't mention that we talked."

"Thanks," Michael answered, walking toward the door. Leaving Greg's office, Michael took a detour to Stephan's department, but he hadn't arrived yet. Walking back to his own office, Michael got to work, excitement coursing through him. He met with various team members, still wondering after each meeting if this was the last time he'd see them. This whole situation was unsettling, and he found he was putting things off, which was something he never did. At lunchtime, Stephan came to his door like he usually did, and they went to lunch, but didn't say much, and afterward they went back to their work areas. Michael promised he'd call as soon as he heard anything. He went ahead and put together the agenda for the weekly project meeting that was scheduled for the following day, but decided not to send it out until he'd heard something. Even the most mundane task or conversation seemed to add to his feeling of impending doom.

"Michael." He looked up and saw Greg standing in his doorway. "Would you come to my office for a minute?" Michael nodded and got up, following him down the hallway. Greg shut the door behind him. "Mark, Michael is here with me."

"Good," he heard through the phone. Michael sat down, wondering just what was going on. "Greg called me this morning to say he'd heard things that didn't make him very happy. I'm not going to go into the source of that information, but I'll leave it at the fact that Greg chewed me out up one side and down the other for a number of reasons." Michael looked up at Greg, who smiled back at him. "So together, Greg and I have decided some things, and they involve you. First, Greg has requested that you stay in Europe until the project is done on temporary assignment to him, and I've agreed. For the duration of this project, you will report to Greg. For the other projects you've retained, you will report your progress directly to me."

Michael smiled, and Greg stood up from his desk, nodding to him before leaving the room, closing the door behind him. "Is Greg gone?" Mark asked.

"Yes," Michael answered, wondering what was going on.

"Greg brought an issue to my attention and was gracious enough to let us use his office to discuss it privately. I have to tell you that I'm a little disappointed that you didn't tell me that you thought Curtis had problems with you because of your sexual orientation. You know you can discuss anything with me."

"I didn't really realize he had, to tell you the truth. I thought he treated everyone the way he treated me," Michael answered, and the other end of the line went completely silent. "I didn't know any different and just thought he wasn't happy with the job I was doing. I couldn't prove anything." Michael was way too happy with the arrangement Mark had described to really care about it too much, anyway.

"Do you think this arrangement will be beneficial?"

"Yes," Michael responded with a smile.

"Good. I'll have Grace set up a weekly call so we can review the progress of your projects and keep the lines of communication open. I also understand that you've requested a week's vacation in Europe, and I know it hadn't yet been approved. As long as it fits your project schedule, I'm fine with it and will approve it today."

"Thanks, Mark," Michael muttered, his mouth still hanging open at the reversal of fortune. "I appreciate it."

"We'll talk soon. Now I have to go handle Curtis's latest problem," Mark added before hanging up, and Michael silenced the dial tone of the speaker phone before opening the door and leaving Greg's office in a surprised daze.

"Is that what you wanted?" Greg asked as Michael passed him in the hallway just before breaking into a grin. "I think you should tell Stephan." Greg winked and patted his shoulder without saying anything more, before heading back into his office. Michael wandered through to the marketing department and saw Stephan lift his head, a questioning look on his face. Michael smiled, nodded, and saw the worry slip from Stephan's face until he, too, was smiling. They couldn't talk with everyone else in the department looking at them, so Michael nodded and left, knowing that Stephan would come to his office when he could.

He didn't have long to wait. Stephan stopped by, and Michael told him everything, after closing the door, of course. "So this means you get to stay?" Stephan asked excitedly.

"Yes, I get to stay," Michael answered, wishing he could share Stephan's enthusiasm. This decision was only a temporary reprieve, after all. When the project was over he'd still have to go home, and Michael wasn't so sure he'd leave either of their hearts intact when he did. He couldn't say anything to Stephan about that right now. The man looked so happy that Michael let himself go with it. They had about four months before that happened, and Michael decided he was going to pull a Scarlett O'Hara and worry about that tomorrow. "Would you like to go somewhere for dinner to celebrate?"

Stephan made a show of thinking about it. "Why don't you come to my apartment, and I'll cook for you."

"I'd like that," Michael answered. He'd been curious about Stephan's place. He'd learned from other Americans in the office that being invited to someone's home was a huge deal, and up to now, Stephan had always come to his hotel room or to the apartment, but for some reason Stephan had never invited him to his home. That he did now had a lump forming in Michael's throat. "I'd love to see where you live." Michael stared across the office at Stephan, losing himself momentarily in deep chocolate eyes. He wanted nothing more than to walk around his desk, take Stephan into his arms, and taste those red lips before devouring his mouth. But he couldn't—not here. A soft knock on the door broke the spell, and Michael saw Stephan blink a few times as if he, too, were realizing where he was.

"Come in," Michael said and saw the door open, Greg sticking his head in.

"Can we talk for a while? I have some questions, and I'd like it if we could go over some project details," Greg said, looking at Stephan and then back at him. "Is half an hour okay?"

"Perfect, I'll come to your office then?"

"No, I'll come here. That way you'll be sure to have everything you need." Greg smiled before leaving again.

"When you're ready to leave, meet me at my desk, and you can follow me," Stephan said before leaving the office. Michael looked after him for a few seconds, seeing Stephan's tight butt over and over until he made his mind focus on the task at hand, and he got to work, getting his documents together for the meeting with Greg. Sending documents to the printer, he forced his mind onto the tasks at hand rather than to what he would be doing after work.

Greg showed up a half hour later, Michael handed him a small packet of papers, and the two men went over the plans in detail. Greg knew the high-level plans already, so it was just a matter of filling in the details. "This looks great," Greg said when they were done. "The only issue I see is what if the software company doesn't deliver? Or worse, what if they deliver crap? There isn't any leeway in the schedule."

"I know, but in order to meet the dates promised, there wasn't any choice. I've been keeping a very close eye on them for that reason, and as of Monday, they were on schedule and had delivered some initial code for review. It wasn't quite where it needs to be, but they are on the right track. I was actually able to see the basics when I was in the office last week," Michael explained. Greg's concerns were the same concerns Michael had had for weeks. "I'll be frank with you. If there is a problem with the project, it will either be in the delivered code or the changes to the host systems that are being made for the accounting. Those are unique to Europe and quite complicated."

Greg agreed, and they continued talking for a while, working through a schedule for weekly updates. Michael was pleased when Greg told him that his door was always open. They both had their concerns, but agreed that there was nothing they could do to mitigate them other than to keep monitoring their progress.

When they were done, Greg left the office, and Michael went back to his plans. After working for half an hour, he realized he was smiling and that he hadn't understood how much he missed being truly happy at work. He hadn't felt that since Dennis's departure, and with Curtis off his back, he could really do his job without worrying about all the drama and crap that Curtis brought to his day. Now he just had to deliver and keep his mind on the project, which seemed to be the one thing that kept getting harder and harder. With Devon and the other guys he'd dated, his job had come first, but with Stephan, those priorities had been turned on their head, and he knew he needed to find his balance quickly or he'd lose focus on what he was sure was quickly becoming the most important project of his career.

Forcing everything from his mind, Michael dug into his work, deciding he needed to make up for his distraction earlier in the day—and he still had other projects that needed to be managed.

A knock on his door pulled him out of his concentration. Looking up, he saw it was nearly six o'clock. Stephan stood in the doorway, looking at him. "I just need a few minutes to finish this up and we can go," Michael said as he typed away, finishing the e-mail and then pressing send before powering down his laptop.

Michael gathered his things, leading Stephan out to the parking lot. "Where should I go?"

"We'll cross the river and turn left near the hotel you were staying at," Stephan explained.

"Then I'll follow you," Michael responded before getting into his car. He waited until Stephan's Smart Car pulled out of its spot before following the tiny car out onto the street and through town. Luckily, the few lights they had to go through didn't separate them, and Michael turned off the main street, following Stephan down a quiet road before they turned again onto a tree-lined residential street with small homes.

Michael waited for Stephan to park and pulled in behind him. Getting out, he followed Stephan to the front of the largest house on the street. "Is this yours?"

"I rent the upstairs," Stephan explained as he pushed open the gate to a meticulously maintained yard filled to bursting with flowers. "The lady who owns the house lives on the first floor. She's older, and I help her maintain the house." Stephan waved toward the front, and Michael saw the curtains move. Stephan led them through the yard and around the side to a door that he unlocked. "Be careful on the stairs. They're very narrow," Stephan cautioned before opening the door and motioning Michael inside.

The stairs upward were indeed narrow and steep, with no railing in sight. Michael climbed slowly, hearing Stephan closing the door behind them before following him up. At the top, Michael stepped to the side, literally leaning against the wall, and let Stephan slide by so his host could show him inside.

The stairway opened into a small living area with a chair, loveseat, and television, a single small wooden cube acting as a table near the chair. Large windows overlooked the front garden. "The kitchen is here, and the bedroom is through that door," Stephan explained. All the rooms were smaller than the ones in Michael's apartment, but every inch of space seemed to have been used to the fullest, as did the furnishings, which were clean and modern. "This is wonderful," Michael commented, almost to himself. "It's so bright and cheerful."

"I know it's much smaller than you're used to," Stephan commented softly.

"It's perfect," Michael said, looking at Stephan, who smiled, and suddenly the room was way too big with Stephan on the opposite side of it. "It's just like you," Michael said as he took a step toward Stephan, locking his gaze on to his lover's eyes, "tidy, small, and beautiful." Michael swallowed as he stood right in front of Stephan, watching his eyes watch him. Raising his hand, he touched Stephan's cheek, stroking the skin. His movements seemed like they were happening in slow motion, the touch of Stephan's cheek, Michael's thumb rubbing a plump lip, the silky softness of his fingers through Stephan's hair. "Thank you for letting me visit your home." Michael leaned forward, their mouths inching toward each other's, and when their lips touched, he heard Stephan gasp softly, like he'd been shocked. The kiss deepened quickly, but Michael made no move to touch him other than with his lips, his hands falling to his side. He felt Stephan lighten the kiss, his lover smiling and then pulling back.

"I'm glad you like it," Stephan told him before turning toward the kitchen. "I should make dinner."

"Can I help?"

Stephan chuckled. "There's barely enough room for one person. We'll probably trip over each other's feet if we both try to cook. Please turn the chair and sit down—you can talk to me while I work, okay?" Michael complied, and Stephan went to work.

They did indeed talk while Stephan moved through his tiny kitchen. Michael watching his lover's body, the movements almost graceful, no motion wasted. Scents that made Michael's mouth water began filling the rooms, and he was tempted to get up and see what was cooking. "Do you like to cook?" Michael asked.

"Yes. My mother wanted me to be a chef. She always said that was a very noble profession. From an early age, she taught me and my sisters how to cook, but I'm the only one who ever really got good at it." Stephan continued moving, and Michael heard the hiss of something searing and smelled the enticing aroma of cooking meat and garlic. "They can both feed themselves and follow a recipe."

"While you can develop your own recipes," Michael finished, and he saw Stephan's head of long, black hair nod. "I wish I'd learned to cook well," Michael continued. "I was never very good at it. I can heat things up or nuke them, but don't ask me to make anything from scratch." More searing sounds came from the kitchen, and the aroma increased as Michael's stomach rumbled.

"Would you like some wine?" Stephan asked, pulling a bottle out of a cupboard and setting it on the counter. "I have a nice red to go with dinner. Is that okay?"

Michael got out of the chair, stepping behind Stephan, slipping his arms around his waist. "It's perfect, just like you." Michael kissed Stephan's neck before backing away so his host could finish cooking.

Stephan felt so good in his arms, and every time he touched him, Michael could feel his heart race with anticipation. As soon as his hands slipped away from Stephan's waist, Michael had the urge to put them back.

"Dinner will be ready soon," Stephan told him, turning from the stove to look at him.

"Are you staring?" Michael asked when he didn't turn away. Stephan nodded and then went back to work.

It wasn't long before plates and dishes were set on the table against the wall that divided the kitchen and living room. There was only room enough for two, but like everything else, it fit. Stephan pulled out the chairs, and Michael sat down, his plate, wine glass, and silverware in front of him, with Stephan taking the chair across the table. "This smells heavenly," Michael commented, inhaling deeply. Stephan smiled at the compliment and slowly began to eat. Michael did as well, and the scent didn't do justice to the flavor. They talked a little between bites, but Michael's thoughts kept intruding.

"I think we need to talk," Michael said once their plates were empty, and he saw some of the light dim in Stephan's eyes.

"Does that mean the same thing in your country that it means here?" Stephan inquired very tentatively.

"I don't know what it means here, but to me it means we need to talk." Michael swallowed, adjusting the way he was sitting on the chair. "We found out today that I'm staying, and I'm happy about that, I really am, but I want to make sure you understand that I'll still have to leave in about four months."

Michael got off the chair, walking to where Stephan was still sitting, placing a hand on his shoulder. "I know I've been somewhat reticent, and that's because I was afraid of how I was going to feel when I went home. I was afraid that my feelings for you would grow and that I wouldn't be able to return home with my heart intact. But that doesn't matter now, because that's not going to happen no matter what. I know that." Michael felt his throat go dry and his heart race as he plowed ahead. "But it wouldn't be fair to you if I didn't give you the chance to back away." Michael felt a touch of fear wrench his stomach. Yes, he knew their time together was probably limited. "We'd still be friends, and I'd never hold it against you," Michael added as he let his hand fall back to his side.

"Is this your way of leaving me?" Stephan asked, speaking to his empty plate.

"No. I'd rather have the next four months with you knowing I'll have to leave—knowing that at the end, my heart will probably break as soon as I get on that plane. I'd rather have what time I can with you than nothing at all. You are worth the chance of complete and total heartbreak. But it's not just *my* heart we're talking about," Michael added, his voice deepening with emotion as he reached down to take Stephan's hand. Holding Stephan's hand in his, Michael stroked the back of it with his thumb, afraid to look into Stephan's eyes, because if he did, he really expected to see rejection. He couldn't blame Stephan for wanting to protect his heart from what was inevitably coming. Michael would eventually have to go home—there wasn't any way around that, at least not one he could see now.

He felt Stephan get out of his chair, and their hands slipped apart. Stephan didn't say anything, and Michael turned toward the front windows, looking out as he gave Stephan some time to think, but as the time went on, he started to wonder if he shouldn't just leave and give Stephan some privacy. He nearly jumped when he felt hands on his waist, and slowly he turned to peer into Stephan's beautiful eyes.

"I'd rather love you for the next four months knowing you have to leave than to turn off my heart and miss out on what could be the best months of my life." Stephan's voice broke as he said the words, and Michael pulled him into a hug as his heart restarted, and the breath he'd been holding slipped from his lungs. How Michael was ever going to let Stephan go when he had to go home, he had no idea, but he had him now, and he loved him. Michael knew that now, and he was going to make damned sure he showed Stephan how he felt at every possible opportunity, starting right now.

Bringing their mouths together, Michael kissed Stephan with everything he had, letting his relief, and yes, his love, flow to him. He'd told Stephan that he loved him in a roundabout way, and that would have to do for now because he didn't feel like talking anymore. When the kiss broke, Michael inclined his head toward the closed door that Stephan had indicated was his bedroom, asking silent permission to take him there. Stephan nodded and moved toward the door, turning the knob and letting Michael enter.

The room was as small as the rest of the apartment, but equally clean. However this room showed more of Stephan's personality than any other room in the apartment. Pictures hung on the walls, and the quilt on the bed looked handmade. Michael didn't ask questions or comment; he simply let Stephan guide them to the bed. "Can I make love to you?" Michael asked as he lifted Stephan's shirt, pulling it over his upraised arms. Stephan nodded as Michael opened his pants, letting them pool at Stephan's feet. "Take off your shoes and lie on the bed," Michael told Stephan, his lips right next to his. "I want to show you just what you mean to me." Michael saw Stephan swallow, and he stepped out of his pants, climbing naked onto the bed. "Do you have any lotion or oil?"

Stephan nodded and pointed to the bathroom. Michael went inside and found a bottle of scented lotion on the counter. Taking it back into the bedroom, Michael set the container on the table before stripping out of his clothes and climbing on the bed, straddling Stephan's body just under his butt. Squirting some of the lotion on his hands, Michael warmed it before placing his hands on Stephan's back. He felt Stephan jump slightly and then he started massaging Stephan's muscles, letting his hands convey all the feelings that mere words just couldn't. With every caress, his hands made love to Stephan through the simple act of touch. Michael knew putting your hands on another person and then being trusted enough for them to give themselves to you could be just as intimate as the actual act of joining with another person.

Stephan's back muscles twitched beneath Michael's fingers, and he increased the pressure, using his palm to stroke and work away the tension. "Let it go," Michael cooed softly, "let all the tension drift away. Let me love you like this." Michael felt the exact moment when Stephan gave himself completely to his care. He exhaled for what seemed like forever, and Michael could feel the knots in Stephan's muscles untie and drift away. Stroking with long, sure movements, Michael transitioned from Stephan's back to his neck and shoulders, caressing the skin as he worked the muscles. "Close your eyes, breathe in and out, give yourself to me," Michael whispered as he shifted on the bed, his hands drifting down Stephan's hip to his leg and all the way down to his feet. Michael worked first one leg and then the other, foot, calf, quad, thigh, letting his hands soothe the muscles, giving his lover a bit of his own energy and care.

Once he was done, he debated having Stephan roll over, but his lover seemed so relaxed that he nixed that idea and knelt on the bed, watching his beautiful lover drift near sleep. Putting more lotion on his hands, Michael slid his hands up the back of Stephan's legs to his butt, massaging a cheek, his hands kneading the muscles. "M... M... Michael," Stephan whimpered as he pushed back against Michael's hands. Michael let them slip away, denying Stephan his touch. Watching, he saw Stephan turn his head, deep eyes filled with desire, staring at him. Stephan's hand moved toward him, and he felt Stephan's fingers touch his cock ever so softly, as though he were asking permission, then fingers curled around his length, holding him. They didn't move, just held him, and Michael nearly growled in frustration before closing his eyes, taking a deep breath and releasing it. He expected patience from Stephan, and he couldn't deny it when Stephan asked it of him.

Michael continued his massage for a few seconds more before he could take it no longer. Slipping his fingers down Stephan's crease, he skimmed over his lover's opening and felt Stephan's fingers tighten around him. Michael's cock jumped, and he had to keep his own lustful desire from running away from him. "Is this what you want?" Michael asked, putting a finger against Stephan's small entrance, teasing, but not pressing inside.

Stephan nodded slowly. "Michael, please," Stephan pleaded, and Michael smiled when he didn't press back, but he could feel the tension in Stephan's hips as though he were forcing himself not to. Smiling at the effort, Michael massaged the skin of Stephan's opening, getting a high-pitched moan in response. Slowly, carefully, Michael sank his finger into Stephan's tight opening, listening to the now deeper, more throaty sounds as Stephan got what he wanted. Michael tapped Stephan's hip, and his lover lifted his butt into the air. Michael slid his other hand between Stephan's legs, caressing the length of his lover's leaking cock.

"You're so beautiful," Michael told him, wondering just how he would ever be able to let this incredible, hedonistic man go. Stephan was so vocal, leaving no doubt as to just what Michael was doing to him and how much he loved it. No subterfuge, no games—just simple, open, honest attraction and pleasure.

"So are you, Michael, the most beautiful man I know."

Michael let his hand slide away, his finger pulling out of Stephan's hot body. Tapping Stephan's hip, Michael watched as he rolled over. Michael wished he had a condom close at hand, not wanting to break contact with Stephan. He watched as his lover reached to the small night table, pulling open a drawer. Michael grabbed one of the condoms inside and opened the packet, rolling it onto himself. Locking eyes with Stephan, Michael placed Stephan's feet on his shoulder and slowly entered his lover's welcoming body.

Heat surrounded him like nothing he'd experienced before. Michael knew the difference was in his feelings for the incredible man he loved. He could admit it now. He loved Stephan, and every second he spent with him, he felt that love grow deeper, blossoming in his heart like a rose. Sliding deeper, joining their bodies, Michael leaned forward, touching their lips together. "I love you, Stephan," he whispered, their lips so close he could feel their breath mingling.

"*Ik hou van je*," Stephan replied before wrapping his arms around Michael's neck, pulling him into a hard kiss that told him in no uncertain terms that no matter the words used, Stephan had just told Michael he was loved too.

Their bodies seemed to move of their own accord after that, each expressing through kisses and movements what the other meant to him. Michael had never experienced anything as wonderful as knowing he was truly making love to another person and how quickly Stephan had opened his heart. Their love and passion built so quickly it stunned him, as Michael came in a blinding flash, his love pulsing into Stephan as his body convulsed his passion around him.

When Michael came back into himself, he was lying on the bed next to Stephan, listening to their deep breathing. All he remembered was their passion and the mind-blowing release it generated. Neither of them moved for quite a while, and it was only the bed shaking that pulled him out of his reverie. Michael turned his head, watching as Stephan padded to the bathroom, returning with a smile and joining him on the bed. Michael removed the condom and disposed of it before holding his dear man close as they kissed languidly, lovingly, worries about the future fading to nearly nothing. "What was it you said to me?"

Stephan wriggled slightly as he moved closer. "*Ik hou van je* is 'I love you' in Dutch." Stephan began tracing his finger over Michael's chest. "*Ik hou van je*," he wrote, and Michael took his fingers, brought them to his lips, and kissed them.

"*Ik hou van je*, Stephan," Michael said haltingly before Stephan smiled and kissed him.

"I love you too."

# CHAPTER
## Ten

THE past six weeks or so had been one of the best times Michael could ever remember. He and Stephan had spent a lot of time together, and Michael found himself falling for the man more and more. They'd gone to the office picnic together and had an absolute ball. Stephan picked him up and drove them to Efteling, a nearby amusement park. The park was amazing—beautifully landscaped, and the buildings were as magical as any elf could possibly imagine. They entered the park and wandered down curving lanes, past leaning buildings and giant toadstools. Elf characters greeted every visitor, and Michael got Stephan's picture sitting next to them in the middle of a magical-looking garden. After wandering on, they passed rides and attractions, and Michael stopped short, his mouth dropping open as he blinked twice. "Does that mean what I think it means?" he asked, completely dumbfounded, before glancing over to Stephan, who looked as though he were about to laugh.

"Yes, I think it does." Stephan chuckled, leading him toward a pavilion with what looked like a grass-thatched roof.

"Oh my freaking God," Michael murmured in near disbelief. "There's no way they could do this in the States. People would protest and boycott the park."

Stephan humphed under his breath before staring at him in disbelief and commenting, "You Americans are so sensitive. Monsieur Cannibale has been here for years." Stephan grabbed his hand and pulled him into the line.

"I can't believe you're taking me on the cannibal ride," Michael commented as they got in line, figuring there was no one who would believe him when he told them about this. The attraction was like the teacup ride at Disneyland, except instead of teacups, you rode in stewpots with huge smiles on them and cartoon flames beneath. The whole ride was presided over by a cartoony pygmy man with a bone through his nose, wearing a chef's hat and holding a large wooden spoon, surrounded by an ice cream cone, tropical fruit, and God knew what else. "This has got to be the most politically incorrect amusement park ride in the history of the world," Michael commented as he leaned on the rail, watching the brightly colored stewpots whirl around and around, the entire thing accompanied by sounds of some modernistic version of tribal drums.

Stephan simply shook his head like Michael was off his nut as the line moved forward, and they just missed the cutoff. Around and around the stewpots went in front of them while the cannibal waited for his dinner. The whole thing was completely, inappropriately, tackily, laughingly, and ridiculously, fun. Their turn came and they filed on, grabbing a red stewpot. Another couple got in with them, and the ride began. They whirled and twirled their way through their turn as the cannibal's dinner before stumbling off the ride, with Michael laughing to beat the band. Once he could see straight, he snapped a few pictures just to be able to prove to his friends that he hadn't gone completely crazy when he told them about it.

He and Stephan spent the rest of the day wandering through the park, riding the amusements and roller coasters. They joined everyone for a to-die-for buffet lunch that would rival the best Sunday brunch buffet in any fine US hotel. But nothing topped the cannibal ride.

For the past month, Michael's project had gone amazingly well, with obstacles arising and their solutions relatively easily found. The few more complicated issues were immediately tackled by the team. Michael knew part of that was due to Mark and Greg's support and interest. Michael made the most of their support that he could, knowing it would remain until the next issue or crisis pulled their attention away.

The first week in July, Michael went back to the States for a week, then returned to Europe as planned. The entire week he'd been in the

Pennsylvania office, Curtis had refused to speak to him in any way, even going as far as to duck into people's offices for impromptu conversations rather than greet him in the hallways. Michael didn't really care what the homophobic weasel did. He was only making himself look bad, and from the few comments he heard from the staff, they saw it, too, and his behavior wasn't winning Curtis any friends.

The next week, Michael was on vacation. He hadn't decided what he was going to do, but he wanted to see things. He couldn't decide if he wanted to take day trips or drive a greater distance. He'd been so busy that he really hadn't had much of a chance to plan.

"Hey, Michael," Greg called from his office door, "are you excited about your vacation?"

"Yes," Michael responded with a smile, "but I haven't decided what I want to do. It's sort of that kid-in-a-candy-store mentality. There's so many things to choose from, I can't decide. I thought about Paris, but realized I didn't need to go that far to see wonderful things, though I'm still not sure."

"Is Stephan going with you?" Greg asked him in a teasing tone, letting him know that their relationship wasn't a secret. Not that Michael ever thought it was, especially when one of the young ladies from accounting had told him once at lunch that she thought he and Stephan made a cute couple. He didn't even know who she was, but after she'd said that, she'd giggled and covered her mouth like she'd said something she knew she shouldn't.

"I asked him," Michael answered, and Greg nodded, walking on as Michael got back to work. The real reason he hadn't made plans was he was still hoping that Stephan would be able to go with him, but he hadn't gotten approval from his supervisor, who had been out of the office on his own vacation. Kai was returning today, and hopefully Stephan would have an answer soon. Michael kept working, but found he had one eye on his keyboard and the other on the door.

Stephan popped his head in a while later. "Kai approved my holiday time," Stephan told him, a happy smile on his face. "Have you decided where you would like to go?" Stepping into the office, Stephan closed the door, his smile fading slightly. "I have to spend some time with my family, though. I called my mother last night, and she asked me to visit." The look on Stephan's face told him that the request was probably issued more like a command. "I told her I was traveling with someone, and she invited you to come too." Stephan looked toward the floor, shifting nervously from foot to foot.

"Do your parents know you're gay?" Michael asked suspiciously, wondering what had Stephan so nervous.

"Yes. I have told them. But they have never extended an invitation to my friends to visit." Stephan raised his head. "I told them you were more than a friend, and she asked me to tell her about you. Then she asked me to bring you."

"Then what's got you so nervous?" Michael wanted to take Stephan into his arms, but refrained since they were in the office.

"I've told my mother about some of my boyfriends, and she has never invited any of them before. She always says that she does not want to know."

"She's your mother, and she loves you and wants you to be happy."

Stephan forced a smile. "Yes, she does, and she thinks she knows what will make me happy—and that is always what will make *her* happy. Since I am the only boy, she says I must get married and have babies."

Michael took a deep breath and made a decision. "Please tell your parents that I would be happy to meet them." *God, he was probably going to regret this.* He thought about asking if there was a hotel nearby where he could stay. While he would probably be more comfortable, Michael knew it would be very rude, and he also knew that being invited to visit was a bit of an honor. "And I'll do my best to make a good impression. Do you know when you want to go?"

Stephan shook his head. "Can we talk tonight?"

"Of course," Michael said. He wanted to say something to reassure Stephan that everything would be okay, but a knock on the door interrupted them. Stephan wiped the nerves from his expression and opened the door, nodding to Greg as he left. Michael answered Greg's questions, and he left the office. Michael went back to clearing his e-mail. The latest note was one from Marty, the development coordinator at the software company that was making the register modifications. Opening it, he saw a note addressed to Curtis but sent to him. Michael figured it was a mistake. The e-mail simply said, "Enclosed are the updated software delivery dates based upon the latest prioritization of projects." Michael opened the attached spreadsheet and almost immediately saw that the delivery dates for the critical software for the Shoe Finder project had been pushed back a month. Instead of an early August delivery, the changes were now scheduled for September.

"Are you okay?" Rocco, the documentation specialist asked as he walked into the office. "You look ready to kill someone."

"I may have to," Michael answered, feeling his anger and frustration build.

"I can come back later," Rocco told him, moving toward the door.

Michael took a deep breath. "Sorry," he told his visitor. "How can I help you?"

Rocco handed him the draft of the system documentation, asking him some questions for clarification. Michael answered him with as much patience as he could muster. It wasn't Rocco's fault that everything was suddenly going to hell. Once Rocco left, Michael opened his timelines and adjusted the dates for software delivery. Just as he suspected, the change in dates would blow his timeline all to hell, and they wouldn't be able to finish the project before the Christmas selling season started. "Fuck," Michael said under his breath. He did not want to tell Greg the bad news but he knew he had to.

Stephan walked in and sat in one of the chairs, looking at him expectantly. "Oh God, I'm sorry," Michael said as he remembered the meeting he'd scheduled with marketing to review the store promotional materials.

"Kai had another meeting and asked me to go over the plans with you," Stephan said very professionally, and then his expression softened. "Something's wrong," he stated, and Michael nodded before explaining what had happened.

"We knew this was a possibility, but last week's update said they were on track to deliver as planned with no current issues. I should have known it was too good to be true." Stephan walked behind the desk, and Michael pulled up the e-mail. "I need to check the last schedule I received in case I made a mistake," Michael said, thinking out loud.

"You didn't," Stephan answered definitively. "You're too careful for that." Michael smiled at Stephan's faith in him. Stephan leaned closer, peering over his shoulder at the screen, reading the e-mail. "Did he send this to you by mistake? It's addressed to Curtis."

"I guess so," Michael answered before showing Stephan the revised implementation dates. "I have to print this out and take it to Greg. He's going to spit nails when he sees this."

Stephan turned his head away from the screen to look at him. "Do you want me to go with you?"

Michael stopped his hands on the keyboard, wondering at such a strange question. He didn't need his hand held. Looking into Stephan's eyes, he saw only concern. "No. I doubt he'll be angry with me." Michael printed copies of the file and e-mail before getting up from his chair and walking toward the door, stopping before he reached it. "Thank you, though, I appreciate the support." Stephan nodded as he followed behind Michael in the hallway. "I'm sorry about our meeting, but this is probably going to take the rest of the day to figure out."

"I'll send you the materials, and we can review it with Kai sometime tomorrow," Stephan said before turning down the hallway toward the marketing department, while Michael grabbed his printouts and headed toward Greg's office, dreading the message he was going to be delivering.

Obed was in Greg's office, and both of them looked up when Michael knocked on the doorframe. Obed got up, but Michael nodded slowly, and he sank back into his chair. "This affects us all, I think." Michael took the other chair, handing Greg a copy of the e-mail. "I received this from Marty. I don't know if he sent it to me on purpose or by accident. But it seems the date for the delivery of our software has shifted back by almost a month." Michael handed Greg a copy of the software-delivery schedule. "I don't know what caused this change, but it puts the entire project in jeopardy. Have you heard anything from Curtis or Mark?"

Greg shook his head, saying nothing as his face got redder and redder. "If I didn't know better," Greg started and then stopped. "I can't say that," Greg muttered before turning to Michael. "We're not supposed to have this, are we?"

Michael shook his head. "I'm starting to think that Marty sent this to me on purpose, but I don't want to get him in trouble."

Greg nodded but said nothing as he thought for a while. "If Marty sent this to you on purpose, then he must think that Curtis is pulling something, or trying to."

Greg leaned forward, dialing a number on his phone and placing it on speaker. Michael heard Curtis answer. "I've got Michael and Obed here with me, and we're making some final implementation preparations for the Shoe Finder rollout. I understand that the store software is on track, and I wanted to check to make sure everything was still going as planned."

"It certainly is. Software development is on track and scheduled for delivery the first week in September."

Greg paused, looking at the sheet Michael had given him. "We've been planning on software delivery the first week in August. What changed?" Michael smiled as the question was met with momentary silence.

"Nothing. We were always planning for September code delivery."

Michael leaned forward to dispute what Curtis was saying, but Greg held up his hand to stop him. "All the project plans, including the ones we have from when you were responsible for the project, show an August 1 code delivery. I expect you to get the tasks back on track. I don't know what happened, but we will not allow a month delay on the tasks you are responsible for." Greg's temper was rising.

"It's not my fault the plan for the project was faulty," Curtis countered, "and there isn't enough time to get the code delivered by then. Early September is really the best we can do." Michael could almost see Curtis's smug smile in his voice. Greg stared daggers at the speaker phone but said nothing more. Greg motioned to both him and Obed to leave the office. They got up, and Michael heard Greg take the phone off speaker as Michael closed the door.

Michael walked back to his office without looking at or talking to anyone, upset and angry, while feeling completely helpless at the same time. Opening his plans, Michael checked everything to make sure he hadn't made a mistake. He couldn't find any. Checking his signoffs, he saw Curtis's along with everyone else's on the plan. As much as he wanted to ram the whole thing down the weasel's throat, he still had to work with the man.

"You okay?" Stephan asked softly from the doorway. "I can come back later, but Greg really needs to go over the materials today."

"That's fine," Michael responded before getting up and moving to one of the chairs, where they both sat close together.

"Is it going to be okay?" Stephan asked.

"Yes. One way or another," Michael told him, wishing he could truly believe it, but one way or another, things would work out. "Thank you."

Stephan looked confused. "What for?"

"Just being there," Michael answered with a small smile. So much of his life had been lived for his job that he'd never realized just how important and wonderful it was to have someone who supported you no matter if you were right or not. His job was what had mattered, and usually Michael's emotional ups and downs were tied to his successes and challenges, but this was different and so much better. Michael lightly touched Stephan's hand, feeling his warmth, before returning his attention to the business at hand.

Together they reviewed the plans for promoting the new service. "These are great, Stephan," Michael told him. "Very creative and eye catching. The US materials weren't this good."

"You're just saying that," Stephan countered, and Michael let the smile slide from his expression.

"No. I'm not. The signage is colorful, eye-catching, and clever. If this doesn't get people to use the new service, I don't know what will. Now I just have to get the new service installed so we can use all your hard work."

Stephan got up, carrying his materials with him. "I'll see you tonight?" Michael nodded, and Stephan left the office, leaving Michael feeling a little less drained.

"I'm looking forward to it," Michael added softly, for himself. Getting up from his chair, Michael went back to his computer and tried to work. The afternoon had been one hell of a roller coaster, and Michael knew the ride wasn't over yet, especially when Greg strode in with a grin on his face.

"I think I got it," Greg told him, taking the chair Stephan had just vacated before shutting the door. "Curtis is so full of shit, it isn't funny, but Mark seemed to believe him. Anyway, Curtis claimed that they couldn't deliver the code because of the special changes required for Italy. What we agreed to, with Mark's blessing, is to break those changes into a separate software release. That will allow the rest of the code to be delivered in August as planned."

"Greg, that was always the plan," Michael told him, and then the light went on. "Jesus, do you know what just happened?" Greg shook his head. "Curtis manufactured an issue so he could solve it and make himself look good in front of Mark." Michael got up, walking to the other chair. He could see it all so clearly. "Let me guess: he blamed the software company because they couldn't deliver everything, and then he was the one who proposed the solution and miraculously got the software company to agree. And amazingly, their resources got freed up so they could get the work done by the date originally promised."

Greg stared at him, disbelieving. "That's a little nuts, isn't it?"

"I don't think so. Kyle, he's one of the other project managers in the office, he used to tell me that he thought Curtis manufactured issues just so he could solve them. He could never prove it. But I think that's what we just got a dose of." Greg shook his head, still not believing him totally, but Michael could almost see him thinking. "The proof, sort of, is in that note we're not supposed to have. Curtis rearranged the priorities so the developers would have to delay, and then all he had to do was put them back. It makes him look like he was able to pull a rabbit out of his hat, at least as far as Mark is concerned."

"If you're so sure of this, then how do we prove it?" Greg challenged before getting to his feet. "Send me a copy of the note you were sent, and I'll see if I can dig up anything else. If Curtis is really acting like this, then Mark needs to know, but I can't go to him about one of his directors unless I have solid proof." Greg smiled. "And I doubt we're going to find it right away, so you've got a few days until you go on holiday. Just make sure everything is all set for while you're gone, and I'll keep an eye on your former boss for you." Greg winked at him before opening the door and leaving the office.

Feeling much better, Michael updated his plans and sent out the materials for his project meetings. Finally, at the end of the day, Michael found Stephan still sitting in his work area waiting for him, the last person left in his area.

"Should we go out for dinner?" Michael asked, hands touching Stephan's shoulders, massaging them lightly.

"I thought you wanted to decide what we were going to do on our holiday," Stephan said, turning around, deep eyes peering at him.

"I think we can talk and eat at the same time," Michael quipped.

Stephan didn't answer with words, but rather, he took Michael's hand and held it to his cheek. The gentle, almost intimate touch found its way to Michael's heart. Letting the hand slip away, Stephan stood up, shutting down his computer for the night before walking with Michael into the evening twilight.

MICHAEL followed Stephan to his flat, where he got a change of clothes, and together they rode to the small restaurant near Michael's place. It wasn't large, but Michael had found it a few weeks earlier, and it had quickly become his favorite place. It was quiet and sort of country rustic, but their food was wonderful. Michael ordered steak béarnaise, which he found he'd become addicted to, and Stephan had Indonesian chicken.

"I was thinking we could stay close by for our holiday," Stephan said after sipping from his glass of wine. "There are wonderful things to see that don't require a lot of travel. We could go to Antwerp and Brussels. Luxembourg is beautiful, and it has Roman ruins. If you want, we can explore a little of northern Germany."

"Should we make hotel reservations, or just take day trips from here?"

"I think getting hotels would be best—that way we wouldn't spend so much time traveling. We can drive, if you like, or we can just take the train," Stephan said. The conversation paused while the server brought their food.

"I'll put myself in your hands," Michael said, feeling excited about seeing things and spending time with Stephan. He found over the past weeks that he was becoming more and more conscious of the passage of time. He would still be in Europe for a few months, but he could almost feel the hourglass of their time together emptying.

"Is something wrong?" Stephan asked, setting down his fork and staring across the table at him. "If that's not what you want to do on holiday, you just need to say."

"No, it's not that. I like your suggestions," Michael clarified, though Stephan continued staring at him. Michael tamped down his apprehension, continuing with his dinner. He'd always been like this, worrying about things that were months away, letting them cloud his fun for today, but he couldn't help it. That was part of what made him a good project manager, but it tended to pull the fun out of things if he let it. Michael tried not to, but he had trouble shutting it off. Consciously pushing it aside, Michael forced himself to concentrate on Stephan. He knew he was being ridiculous. Stephan was with him right now, sitting just across the table, and all he could worry about was the time months down the road when he would have to leave him behind. They had a vacation to plan and a lot of time to spend with each other. Michael needed to make sure that would be enough, because it had to be.

"At the end of our holiday, we can visit my family, and I can show you where I grew up," Stephan was saying, and Michael pulled his mind back to their conversation. "Oh," he added excitedly, "there's a very old windmill in town, and my father knows the caretaker. He can probably arrange for you to see inside."

"You're kidding?" Michael said with a grin as Stephan nodded emphatically.

At the end of the meal, they paid their bill and walked back to Michael's apartment. Stephan settled on the sofa, and Michael opened a bottle of wine before pouring two glasses and carrying them into the living room. Sitting next to Stephan, Michael leaned against him, soaking in Stephan's warmth as his mind wandered. "Can I ask you something?"

"Of course," Michael answered, nodding slightly against Stephan's shoulder.

Stephan turned to look at him. "Are you happy?"

Michael didn't know quite what to make of the question. But he answered honestly, "Yes." Reaching for his lover, Michael hugged him close, rocking gently. "Yes. You make me very happy."

"You have been quiet, and I thought something was wrong."

"There's nothing wrong." At least nothing he or Stephan could change. "I've just had a lot on my mind lately. I didn't mean to make you feel bad."

"I was just wondering if I'd done something," Stephan said.

Michael took Stephan's glass from his hand, setting it with his glass on the coffee table before standing up and extending his hand. Stephan took it, and Michael turned out the lights as he led Stephan toward the bedroom.

"You haven't done anything except be there when I needed you," Michael told his lover as he tugged the shirt up and over Stephan's head and up-stretched arms. God, he loved the look of Stephan with his arms above his head, all stretched out for him with everything so accessible. Opening his belt, Michael unfastened Stephan's pants before sliding them and his underwear down his legs. Stephan stepped out of them along with his shoes, the stood at the foot of the bed, wearing only his socks. Michael stepped back, just looking at him. "You're beautiful, Stephan, both inside and out." Michael saw Stephan meet his eyes, watching him. Michael reached out, stroking Stephan's arms, then splaying his hands against Stephan's side just under his arms, each thumb caressing a nipple. Stephan shivered, and Michael shifted his hands lower, caressing Stephan's belly as he sucked lightly on Stephan's chest.

"Michael, you make me want," Stephan gasped, and Michael could feel Stephan's legs shaking and his belly quivering. Caressing lower, Michael circled his fingers around the base of Stephan's cock, his fingers sliding through his nest of black curls. Using his other hand, Michael stroked Stephan slowly and deliberately, feeling Stephan's hips move with him.

"You look so sexy, so handsome," Michael whispered, tasting Stephan's skin, swirling his tongue into Stephan's sensitive belly button. Michael had spent hours exploring Stephan's body, and he loved finding the hidden places that made him quiver. "I love you, Stephan," Michael said, looking into Stephan's eyes as he lowered himself to his knees. "Lower your arms and lean back against the bed," Michael instructed, and Stephan slowly let his arms fall, placing them behind him as he leaned back, arching his back. Stephan looked like an offering laid out for him.

Tapping the inside of Stephan's quivering legs, Michael stroked the smooth skin, watching as Stephan's head fell back. Scooting closer, Michael ran his tongue over the head of Stephan's cock. He heard a small gasp as Stephan's rich taste burst onto his tongue. With teasing slowness, he took Stephan deep, judging just what he was doing to him by his whimpers and the way Stephan's legs shook. When Michael took him deep, Stephan would squeak slightly, and his legs quivered with the speed of a hummingbird's wings. When Michael backed away, Stephan's legs settled down. Damn, Michael loved knowing he could affect his lover like this. That he could give Stephan so much pleasure had him throbbing in his own pants, and soon the tightness got to be too much. Pulling away, to Stephan's frustrated groan, Michael pulled off his shirt, shoes thunking as they bounced on the carpet, his pants joining the rest of his clothes on the floor.

"Hands and knees," Michael said as he tapped Stephan's hip. Stephan jumped onto the bed, the mattress bouncing as he hurried to get into position. Michael smiled as he climbed behind him, his own legs shaking as Stephan presented his ass for him. Spreading Stephan's cheeks, Michael ran his tongue along his lover's cleft, teasing the skin for a moment before driving his tongue into Stephan's body, rimming deep and hard. Stephan's ecstatic cry spurred him on, nearly breaking the last of Michael's control. Reaching over to the nightstand, Michael found a condom, his hands fumbling as he ripped the packet open before rolling it on himself. Grabbing the small bottle of lube, Michael hastily applied some to the condom and Stephan. "Not going to be gentle," he warned.

Stephan quivered, replying in Dutch between clenched teeth, and Michael did his best to enter his lover as slowly and carefully as his wavering control would allow. Michael needn't have worried. As soon as he breached Stephan, his lover surged back, impaling himself and driving the breath from Michael's lungs. Once he caught his air again, Michael withdrew and drove himself deep, all caution and control leaving him as instinct and pure, primal need took over. Stephan talked constantly, a steady stream of Dutch that barely penetrated Michael's brain, his cries becoming higher and more shrill. For a second, Michael thought he might be hurting him until he felt Stephan's body tighten around him. Michael rode out Stephan's climax, feeling his lover shake beneath him. Leaning forward, he wrapped his arms around Stephan's chest, pulling him up as he kissed him, driving deep. Stephan was nearly as limp as a rag doll in his arms, and Michael held him tight as his own climax built from the depths of his soul. Telling Stephan just how much he loved him, Michael came deep and hard, filling the condom before allowing them both to collapse onto the bed.

Stephan shifted beneath him, and Michael rolled away, giving him some room. Pulling off the condom, Michael made himself get off the bed to take care of it. Getting a damp cloth while he was at it, he returned to the bedroom, where a naked and very relaxed Stephan lay sprawled on his back, eyes closed, his chest rising and falling. Stephan jumped slightly when Michael wiped his skin with the cloth, drying him with a towel before returning them to the bathroom and then joining his lover on the bed. Stephan curled around him, holding him without opening his eyes.

Closing his own eyes, Michael let his mind float freely, and one idea that had been lingering in the back of his mind for a while kept coming to the surface. "Stephan?"

"Hmmm," he heard his lover mutter softly, eyes remaining closed.

"Do you...?" He stopped himself, knowing it wasn't fair to ask Stephan anything when he was nearly asleep. Michael knew the answer to what had been bothering him was simple—he could look into moving here. But would Stephan really want him here? And what if things didn't work out.... Opening his eyes, he looked at Stephan's face, relaxed and peaceful in sleep, wondering just what he'd say.

Michael lay awake watching Stephan sleep for a while, but couldn't fall asleep himself. The room was warm, so Stephan had rolled away, deeply asleep. Getting up as gently as he could, Michael turned the air conditioner on low to move and dry the air before leaving the room, closing the door behind him.

Michael wandered naked through the dark apartment, closing the curtains more out of habit than a worry that the ducks on the lake would see him. Michael cleaned up the wineglasses, draining his before setting them in the sink. Walking back toward the bedroom, Michael saw his phone on the table. Picking it up and looking through his contacts, he found the number he was looking for and dialed.

"Michael," a familiar deep voice called happily. "How are things in the real Dutch Wonderland?"

"They're doing okay. How's everything there?" Michael settled on the sofa, stretching out in the warm room as the sounds of the night drifted through the open windows.

"Just fine. When will you be back? We both miss you," Jake asked, and Michael heard another phone pick up.

"Is that you, Mikey?"

"Hi, Rog," Michael said.

"So," Jake started taking control of the conversation, "is there something on your mind? I bet there is, and it has to do with that hottie you told us about."

"Yes. There's something I wanted to ask you about Stephan, and I'm not sure how to do it. I've got this problem." Michael wasn't sure how to explain everything.

"Are you in love with him?" Jake asked, all teasing gone from his voice. "God, I can tell you are just by the lost-puppy sound in your voice." A loud sigh came through the line. "Only you would fall in love with a guy who lives three thousand miles away from home. Talk about long distance."

"I know. The problem is that I don't know what to do."

"There's nothing you can do," Roger said, cutting Jake off. "You'll need to come home in a few months, and you'll move on. The other alternative is to distance yourself from him now before you get in too deep, but if I know you, it's probably too late for that."

"Why do you say that?" Michael asked, curious what Roger meant.

But it was Jake's voice that answered. "You've kept your heart closed off for a long time, and now that you've opened it, there's no going back. It's like Pandora's box," Jake told him gently. "We're really happy you found love, but you don't make it easy, do you?"

"Well…," Michael started to say, "I was thinking of finding a job here."

"Oh, please," Jake sniped, his queeniness coming out. "You've been there a little over two months and you're already thinking of moving to be with a guy? That never works out. What about your family? Your parents are getting older. Are you prepared to leave them an ocean away? I know you haven't been exactly close, but they're still your family, and they love you, just like we love you." Jake paused in his rant. "And if you convince Stephan to come back with you, then what about his life and his family? Sorry, I shouldn't get all Baby Jane on you, but we care about you."

"I know you do," Michael answered, feeling very empty and alone. He'd been hoping for support from his friends, not a huge bucket of cold water. What Jake said made sense, and it wasn't as though he hadn't asked himself the same questions.

"I don't doubt your feelings for Stephan," Jake continued, his voice more soothing and quiet. "I really don't. If you're asking these questions, then you really do care for him. Your feelings probably have you all muddled up. I know I got that way when I first met Roger. It's natural, and you shouldn't rush into anything. If you decide to move there to be with him, and this should be a big if at this point, then make sure you're doing it for the right reasons. Make sure you're doing it because it will make you happy."

"Michael, hon, ask yourself this," Roger cut in, his naturally gentle voice a contrast to Jake's usual brashness. "Would you move there if Stephan wasn't in the picture? Do you like it well enough that if they offered you a job, you would take it without Stephan?"

Michael opened his mouth to answer and hesitated, unable to answer the question.

"You've got time," Roger told him. "You don't have to make any decisions now. You've only known Stephan for a few months. Relax, have fun, and see how you get along in the longer term. I know you like to plan out everything, but this is something that can't be planned or analyzed to death to find a single cause or solution. Enjoy what you have instead of worrying about what will happen."

Michael had to admit that what they said made sense. His mind was listening, but his heart wasn't so much. "Thanks, guys. I can always count on the truth, no matter how much it hurts." They talked for a few more minutes before disconnecting. Michael set his phone on the table and walked toward the bedroom door. Opening it, he saw that Stephan hadn't moved at all. The room felt fresher, and Michael closed the door, carefully climbing back in bed. As soon as he did, Stephan curled close to him without waking up.

Michael closed his eyes, trying to settle his mind. He'd hoped calling his friends would help, and it had, sort of. They were right in some ways. He needed to stop worrying about the future and enjoy the now. In a few days, he and Stephan were going away together. That would tell a lot about how well they got along and whether they'd get sick of one another after a prolonged time of being together. Relaxing, listening to Stephan's soft breathing, feeling his touch on his skin, Michael finally let go of his fears and fell asleep.

# CHAPTER Eleven

THE rest of the week was blessedly quiet. Curtis provided no additional drama, and Michael figured that somehow Greg had communicated to him that he wasn't off the hook for the crap he was pulling. When Michael had contacted Curtis with questions, he was suddenly very accommodating.

Friday evening, Michael and Stephan had dinner together, sleeping at Stephan's apartment. "It's way too early for that," Stephan groaned softly, burying his head in the pillow when Michael came out of the bathroom dressed, packed, and ready to go the next morning. "It's only"—Stephan lifted his head to look at the clock—"seven thirty. Good God, we are on holiday." Stephan rolled over, the covers slipping away to reveal his butt, and Michael suddenly reconsidered his stance on the issue, stripping down again. Stephan didn't get back to sleep, but they did spend more time in bed. Later in the morning, Michael got dressed once again while Stephan cleaned up, and after a light breakfast, they packed the car and headed out.

Stephan had booked them into a small, family-run hotel in Beveren, Belgium, a small town outside Antwerp, where they were staying for a few days. Arriving in the early afternoon, he and Stephan explored the historic town and had a nice dinner in the hotel dining room. Michael could feel the tension beginning to seep from his body as he and Stephan wandered the quiet streets of the sleepy town after dark.

The next day, Michael drove into Antwerp, and they toured the city, visiting countless churches with huge, breathtaking art that jumped off the canvases, and of course the Rubens house museum where much of the art they saw had been produced. "This is amazing," Michael mumbled as they entered the largest church yet. Craning his neck, he tried to look everywhere at once before his eye settled on the mammoth altarpiece that the guide sheet they'd purchased said was by Rubens.

"Go take a look," Stephan encouraged, "the backs of the doors are painted as well, so even when it's closed, it's spectacular." When Michael didn't move, Stephan surreptitiously squeezed his hand, and he stepped forward, standing near the foot of the steps, taking in the sheer magnitude of the work before walking around behind to look at the back panels of the doors.

After they'd done the entire walking tour of the city, they found themselves back at the main shopping street. The summer sun warmed them as they window-shopped for a while before Stephan led them to a small park where they lounged in the shade, the breeze rustling the leaves over their heads. "This was a great idea," Michael commented as he sipped from the fresh lemonade they'd bought at a small stand.

"What, the lemonade?" Stephan asked, and Michael was about to explain when he saw Stephan's teasing smile. Michael wanted to kiss that look away, but didn't think that was a particularly good idea in such a public place. "I'm glad you are having a good time."

"How could I not? I'm here with you," Michael replied, thinking *screw it* before bringing Stephan closer for a brief kiss. They sat in the shade awhile longer, cooling off before getting up and walking back to where they'd parked the car. That evening they ate at a small restaurant near their hotel and went to bed, making love for half the night.

The following day, they drove an hour to Brussels, where Stephan had him park the car on the edge of the city, and they rode the subway as they explored the city. Michael marveled at the guild halls surrounding the main square, and they wandered over to see the statue of the little boy peeing, after stopping at Godiva for chocolate, of course. They ate lunch in the Grand Sablon area of the city, where they found a small bake shop that served lunch on tables on the sidewalk. After lunch, they explored some more, taking the subway to the Atomium, the atom structure built for the World's Fair in 1958, before going back to the car. On the way back to the hotel, Stephan directed them to Waterloo battlefield, where Napoleon had met his final defeat. Together they walked to the top of the hill to see the bronze lion cast from the guns of the defeated French. Stephan kissed Michael hard, making them both growl as they stood in the shadow of the huge lion.

They ate late that evening. Wandering around town to settle their stomachs, they came across a carnival a few blocks from the hotel. Michael bought tickets, and he and Stephan had a ball riding the Ferris wheel and the bumper cars. Stephan even convinced him to try one of the games. Michael got the ping-pong ball in one of the colored cups and won a huge stuffed dog. They both laughed as Michael presented it to Stephan. Continuing their exploration of the carnival, Michael saw a little girl dressed in pink, who had to be about four, pointing to Stephan as she talked to a man Michael assumed was her dad. Michael couldn't understand a word of what she was saying, but the tone and the look in her eyes was universal.

Stephan walked over to them as she was practically pulling her dad toward the booth where they'd won the dog. Stephan talked to the father before bending down and handing the dog to the little girl. It was almost as big as she was, but somehow she got her arms around it, hugging the dog tightly as she squealed with delight. Michael wished he had his camera with him. Eventually the father and daughter walked away, the little girl handing the dog to her dad, and she held his hand, turning around to wave good-bye. The smile on her face was the perfect cap to a perfect day.

The following morning, they checked out, driving on to Luxembourg and spending a few days exploring the city and ruins before moving on. They spent the rest of the week in Germany, traveling up the Rhine, continuing north and back into the Netherlands near where Stephan's family lived.

Michael couldn't keep his nerves at bay as Stephan directed him off the freeway and onto smaller roads as they approached the town of Hardenburg. Stephan guided him through town, but Michael barely saw anything except the road. "Do you think your parents will like me?" God, he sounded just like some kid out of high school, and he wished he hadn't asked that.

"My parents are pretty amazing," Stephan explained. "When I told them I was gay, they had a hard time of it at first, but they love me and try to understand."

"Have you ever brought anyone to meet them before?" Michael clutched the wheel, looking over at Stephan as they stopped at a traffic signal. Stephan had probably told him already, but he was too nervous to remember.

"No. I never had anyone I wanted them to meet, before now."

Michael swallowed and tried his best to smile.

"It's green," Stephan told him, and Michael turned his attention back to driving. "My sisters are going to just love you, and so will Mom and Dad. Please do not worry."

"That's easier said than done. Do they speak English?"

"My sisters do, and Mom does a little. Dad not so much," Stephan explained, and Michael rolled his eyes. It was hard enough meeting your lover's parents for the first time, but knowing they didn't speak English was just peachy.

Stephan directed him to turn, and they drove out of town to a quiet, semi-rural area. "When Dad sold the farm, they wanted a place where they could have a garden. Turn left here, it's the second house on the right."

Stephan had him park in front of a relatively large, two-story, tan brick home with fresh, white trim, surrounded by gardens. Architecturally, the home was plain, but it was immaculately maintained—even the walk leading to the door nearly sparkled. Taking a deep breath, Michael opened his door, getting out of the car. He closed his door, peering over the roof of the car as he took everything in while waiting for Stephan. Walking around the car, Michael felt his stomach do a flip-flop as he followed Stephan up the walk.

The front door opened, and a woman in her early sixties waited for them to approach. She opened the door, holding it for them as they entered the house. As soon as the door closed, Stephan was pulled to her and hugged within an inch of his life as his mother greeted him. Michael held back, waiting and looking around the small vestibule. Open stairs led upward next to a small table with the telephone and a chair. Straight ahead was an open archway to what looked like the kitchen. While small, the room had what Michael had come to realize was a very Dutch trait—small spaces didn't feel small because every inch of space was carefully used to its maximum.

Stephan stepped back. "Mama, this is Michael. Michael, this is my mother, Hanna."

Michael expended his hand, saying, "It's very nice to meet you."

"Welcome to our home," she responded in halting English, and Michael smiled.

"*Dank u well*," Michael replied, as she lightly shook his hand. Michael saw her smile at his attempt at Dutch before turning to Stephan. Mother and son spoke for a while, and Michael wondered just what they were saying, until he saw Hanna motion them into the back of the house. Michael followed Stephan and his mother, the two of them jabbering away. While Michael didn't understand a word of what was being said, he did understand that she was a mother very happy to see her son.

Stephan's mother motioned them both to the table. "I make lunch," she told them matter-of-factly, pointing to the table, which was obviously an invitation, or command, to sit down where places had been set. Michael did as he was instructed and waited. Stephan's mother brought bowls of soup, placing one in front of each of them before bringing in plates of bread, meats, and cheese.

"You probably will not like that one." Stephan pointed to slices of deep red meat. "I know you do not eat horse in America. My father loves it, but I can't stand it at all."

Michael nodded, avoiding the meat altogether in favor of bread and cheese as he ate the flavorful soup. It was basic, but good, and when Michael emptied the bowl, Hanna whisked it away as he finished a second piece of the hearty bread. "This is amazing," Michael told Hanna, indicating the cheese. She smiled and nodded. Michael wasn't sure if she understood or not. Once they were done eating—or Hanna determined they were done, Michael wasn't sure which—the plates were taken away and the table cleared. Michael watched Stephan to see what he should do. Stephan got up, and Michael followed him into the living area. Stephan and his mother continued talking as she worked, and Michael did his best to relax, but it wasn't working. For the first time since coming to the Netherlands, Michael felt like a stranger in a strange land.

Stephan's mother came into the room, wiping her hands, and appeared to ask Stephan a question. He answered and she left. "Why don't we take our bags upstairs?" Stephan asked him, and Michael nodded, happy to have something to do. Instead of going through the front again, Stephan led him out through the patio doors. "This is Papa's garden," Stephan told him as he led Michael down a paved path that snaked around the side of the house. "Mama does the flowers and Papa does his vegetables.

"What kind of farm did your parents have?" Michael asked, noticing that even the vegetable garden looked manicured and nearly perfect.

"They grew vegetables of all kinds and also had a small orchard. They had a stand for many years. We all used to help pick and sell the produce, but as they got older it got harder. Papa got the opportunity to sell the land at a very good price a few years ago, then he and Mama retired. The farm was a lot of work, and I am very happy they can enjoy life more now," Stephan told him as they walked around the side of the house to the front yard. Michael opened the trunk and took out their bags before following Stephan back into the house and up the narrow stairs. He had to be careful not to scrape the walls with his suitcase.

Stephan opened a door at the top of the stairs, leading Michael into a bedroom with two twin beds. Michael didn't make any comment whatsoever. He'd determined quite a while ago that he and Stephan wouldn't be able to make love here. Entering the small room, Michael set his case against the foot of one of the beds.

"You're not comfortable here, are you?" Stephan asked, setting down his own bag. Michael shook his head, but said nothing more. Meeting your lover's parents is awkward enough, but not speaking the same language, combined with the different culture and expectations, had Michael on edge.

"I guess I'd have been surprised if I had been," Michael explained. "Please don't worry about it. I know why, and it's no one's fault." It was just the situation; Michael knew that.

Stephan walked to him, standing in front of him. "I love you for making the effort." Stephan leaned closer, his arms snaking around Michael's neck as he brought their lips together in a promising kiss that nearly curled Michael's toes. "*Ik hou van je*," Stephan said softly, and Michael repeated it against Stephan's soft lips.

A soft gasp cut through the room, and Michael turned his head. Stephan's mother stood in the doorway with towels in her hands. She placed them on the nearest bed and hurried away. Michael saw Stephan look at him and then turn toward the now empty doorway and back again. "Go talk to her," Michael told him. "I'll be down in a while." Stephan nodded silently, leaving the room.

Michael looked around the immaculately clean room with its tidy, matching bedspreads. There wasn't a lot of room to move around the beds, but everything seemed to work. From the pictures on the wall, Michael concluded that this room usually belonged to one of Stephan's sisters. Michael kept listening near the door, but heard nothing. Hoping it was safe, he walked down the stairs, being sure to make noise so they knew he was coming. Michael found Stephan and his mother in the living area, sitting together on the sofa. He knew she'd been crying, but she was also smiling at Stephan. When she saw Michael, however, her expression hardened somewhat for a few seconds and then relaxed again. Michael wondered what that was for, but even without the language barrier, it would be nearly impossible to ask without being rude, so he let it drop.

Thankfully, the sound of bells drifted in through the open windows, and Michael saw two women walking bicycles pass in front of the large windows. Stephan said something to his mother before hugging her and jumping to his feet. Michael got up as well, and then heard squeals as the women rushed inside, carrying cloth bags that they set on the table, before alternately hugging Stephan, both of them talking excitedly at the same time. "Stephi, is this your boyfriend?" the taller of the two asked in English with a glint of mischief in her eyes.

"Yes, this is Michael," Stephan said, smiling at him. "Michael, these are my sisters, Allene and Odette. Allie and Odie," Stephan clarified affectionately.

"It's nice to meet you both. Stephan has told me about both of you," he said with what he hoped was a warm smile. Stephan hadn't told him a great deal, but he had mentioned both of them. Hanna said something as she approached the table, and the girls picked up the bags, still talking as they began putting things away.

"How long have you known Stephi?" the taller of the sisters, Odette, Michael believed, asked as she opened one of the cupboards.

Michael started doing the math in his head. "A little over two months, I guess."

"You work together?" Allene asked as she pulled her head out of the refrigerator, closing the door.

"In different departments. I'm a project manager in information systems," Michael answered, watching as cupboards were closed after Odette pulled out glasses and a large bottle of Coke, setting them on the table. Hanna clicked her teeth, something all three of her children ignored as they filled glasses, sitting at the table. Stephan motioned for him to join them, and Michael took a seat. Hanna went into the kitchen and began puttering while the girls peppered him with questions.

Late in the afternoon, Stephan's father, Franz, came home, a small man with gray hair and bright eyes. Introductions were made, but he said very little to anyone, including Stephan, and everyone seemed to take that as normal. The conversation continued, some in English and some in Dutch. It was a weird mix, but managed to include just about everyone, except Franz, who disappeared into his garden shortly after getting home and changing his clothes.

Dinner was surprisingly quiet after the noisy afternoon of talking. Allie set out the plates and silverware while Odie helped her mother bring the food to the table. Franz came in from outside, cleaned up, and sat at the head of the table. Once everyone was seated, they all bowed their heads, and Franz said a soft prayer. No one talked much during dinner, and the conversation that did occur was quiet and brief. Michael made a note to ask Stephan about it, because it seemed so out of character compared to earlier that afternoon. The food wasn't fancy, but it was flavorful and hearty, with an emphasis on vegetables, noodles, and bread. "This is delicious," Michael told Hanna with a huge smile as he cleaned his plate.

"I told you Mama was a good cook," Stephan said, and Michael heard him translate for his mother, who beamed. After dinner, Hanna brought out a bowl of fresh fruit that Michael assumed came from their garden.

With the dishes cleared and the table cleaned, they lingered around the table talking for quite awhile. Most of the conversation was in Dutch, and Michael was happy to sit back and just listen to a family talking about its business. Stephan translated from time to time, but it didn't matter much. Michael was able to pick out the meaning in most things by gestures and facial expressions. As the evening wore on, Franz and Hanna went up to bed, with everyone else following close behind.

Michael took his turn in the bathroom before returning to the room with Stephan, climbing beneath the covers of the twin bed closest to the window. "Is everything okay with your mom?" Michael asked in the dark room.

"Yes. She was shocked, but I think she understands things better now. She told me she loved me," Stephan said softly, and Michael heard Stephan's mattress squeak slightly. A few seconds later, his covers lifted, and Stephan climbed in bed with him. "I can't sleep with you, but we can at least hold each other for a while," Stephan told him, and Michael sighed softly. "Everyone liked you. Allie and Odie think you're handsome and very nice, and you made Mama very happy when you complimented her food."

Michael kissed Stephan, holding him tight. "I hoped I made a few points. She didn't seem to like me very much at first."

"She's worried for me," Stephan said, before giving him another kiss. Slipping from under the covers, Stephan went back to his own bed, and Michael closed his eyes, Stephan's taste still on his lips.

THE following day, Michael, Stephan, and his sisters spent much of the morning and afternoon about town. They did indeed take him to the windmill, and he was given a tour inside, which he found fascinating. This particular piece of history had originally been built to pump water, but had been converted to milling grain. Not that it mattered to Michael—he'd just wanted to see a real windmill. They ate lunch in a small café, with dozens of people stopping to say hello to Stephan and his sisters. They seemed to know everyone, and everyone knew them, and to each person, Stephan introduced Michael with a wide smile. Michael must have shaken more hands than he could ever remember in a single day in his life.

After lunch, they went shopping, and Michael bought his mother a small piece of jewelry made by a local artist. Late in the afternoon, they returned to Stephan's parents' home. Hanna sent the girls on an errand, and they retrieved their bicycles, ringing the bells as they rode away. Franz took Stephan outside with him, and Michael found himself alone with Hanna. He didn't doubt for a second that she'd engineered things this way.

"Sit," she told him, motioning toward the table. Not wanting to be rude and more than a little intrigued, Michael pulled out a chair, and Hanna brought him a glass, pouring him a soda. "We talk," she added, sitting down across from him. To say that Michael was curious about what Hanna wanted was an understatement, but he nodded and waited for her to continue.

"You will go home, yes?" she asked. "To America." Some of her words were the Dutch version, but Michael was able to get the idea.

"Yes," Michael admitted. It was too difficult to explain everything he'd been feeling. "In October." God, he hoped she understood.

She seemed to, because she nodded and continued, but it was very hard for her, and her face showed it. "Stephan," she said, searching for the word, "like…." She shook her head and drew a heart on the table with her finger.

"Love?" Michael questioned, and she nodded.

"Love you."

"And I love him," Michael admitted, as he remembered what she'd seen the day before.

"You go home," she said softly, and Michael understood what she was saying.

He opened his mouth to try to explain things, knowing she wouldn't understand. But he said it anyway. "Yes, I'm supposed to go back to the States, and yes, I'm in love with Stephan, and I don't know what I can do about either one."

The words came out in a rush, and he knew she couldn't follow what he was saying. "I thought about asking him to come with me, but after visiting you, Franz, Allie, and Odie, I can't even do that because it wouldn't be right to take him away from his family and this place. I've been thinking about staying here, but if I stay, am I staying just for Stephan? And if I do, is that enough? Am I putting too much pressure on him? I mean, what if it doesn't work out, but he feels guilty and stays with me anyway? Or worse, what if it doesn't work out at all? My friends say I have time to decide, but that I shouldn't move here just for Stephan. I've been thinking about this for a while and can't figure it out, so if you have any suggestions, I'd like to hear them."

Stephan's mother looked at him like he'd lost his mind before reaching across the table, patting his hand. "You stay."

Michael lifted his eyes from the table, where he'd been looking through his frustrated rant, meeting her eyes. To his surprise, he didn't see condemnation or judgment, just concern, and love for her son. He hadn't known what to expect from Stephan's family, but this wasn't what he'd expected. "I will try," he answered, nodding slowly.

"What are you talking about?" Stephan asked as he stepped inside, handing his mother a basket of fresh vegetables. As Stephan talked to her in Dutch, Michael noticed that Stephan seemed to be asking questions that his mother didn't answer. Instead, she got up from the table, took the basket from Stephan, and gave Michael a nod and look that didn't need any words of explanation.

Stephan looked at him, but he shrugged. There was no way he could explain the conversation he'd just had with Hanna, even to Stephan—especially since he could barely understand it himself, but he felt better. Yes, he still had things he needed to decide, but the answer had been that simple. *"You stay."* Now he just needed to find out if that was what Stephan wanted, or if Michael had been reading everything all wrong. He decided to wait until the drive home to talk it over with him.

"What are we doing tonight?" Michael asked, trying to find something to talk about that would get the confused look off Stephan's face.

"Odie said there's a new dance club in town. She, Allie, and some friends were going to go, and they invited us to go along. Are you interested?" Stephan asked, doing a weird thing with his eyebrows that made him look funny.

"If I agree, will you promise to stop doing that?" Michael teased, and Stephan pouted for a split second before grinning.

"Allie says it's a very young and mixed crowd, and that guys dance together there." Stephan told him, slipping into the chair his mother had vacated. "I think it would be fun to dance with you on the last night of our vacation."

"Are you a good dancer?" Michael inquired, knowing it wouldn't really matter. He'd love to hold Stephan in his arms while they danced. Nothing would make him happier.

"You will have to come tonight to find out," Stephan quipped before giving Michael a wink. "And now I have to go outside to help Papa for a while. It's a beautiful day—you should join us." Stephan got up, and Michael emptied his glass before following Stephan outside.

Michael worked in the garden, helping Stephan tie up tomato plants, for the rest of the afternoon. As he worked, Franz kept looking over to see if he was doing it right, and a few times he actually nodded and smiled. Hanna made an amazing dinner with what Stephan said was veal. He had no idea how she cooked it, but it was wonderful, as was the rest of the meal, and Michael figured Hanna was going all out for her son. After dinner, Stephan and his sisters led Michael out back to the shed. "We won't drive," Stephan told him.

"Yeah," Allie said, chiming in, "if we want to drink alcohol then we have to ride bicycles." She opened the door, and they found a bicycle for each of them. Michael hadn't ridden a bike in years. He was definitely out of practice, and by the time they got to town he was winded and beginning to wonder just how he was going to make it back at the end of the night.

However, as soon as they entered the club, with its music, lights, and energy, those worries slipped away. After some time watching the crowd while having a beer, Michael pulled Stephan toward what appeared to be the boy's section of the club, and they danced. Hips swayed and gyrated to the techno beat. As the evening progressed, the dancing got closer, more intimate, and Michael tugged Stephan to him, their hips grinding together, hands holding each other close as sweat beaded and ran down Michael's skin. He felt exhilarated and totally in love. All doubts and questions danced and ground their way out of his mind. No more doubts and questions—he'd had enough of those.

He needed to speak with Stephan on the way home in the morning, but he also had a number of other people he needed to talk with as well. He knew what he wanted now, and that was Stephan in his arms and in his bed for as long as he'd have him. There was a way, and he knew what it was. Continuing their dance, Michael placed his hand behind Stephan's head, pulling him in for a deep kiss. It didn't matter who was near or who saw, Michael loved Stephan as he'd loved no one else before, and he needed to show it.

# CHAPTER Twelve

THE following morning, after a late night and a hearty breakfast from Stephan's mother, Michael loaded the car, carrying their cases and bags down the stairs while Stephan said good-bye to his family. As Michael reached the bottom of the stairs for the last time, he saw Hanna hugging Stephan tightly, and Michael turned away when he saw Hanna blotting her eyes. Michael put the bags in the trunk and went back inside, where Odie and Allie each said good-bye. Franz shook his hand, and Hanna gave him a hug. He wasn't sure what she said, but he returned her hug before saying a final good-bye.

Michael felt a bit of a lump in his throat as he walked toward the car, and he knew Stephan was probably already missing his family as they pulled away from the house. He didn't need directions, and easily found his way back to the main road with Stephan sitting silently in the passenger seat, staring out the window. "I know you are only going to be here for a few more months," Stephan said, turning to look at Michael.

"I know, and I've been thinking about that a lot."

"Me too, and I was wondering if you thought I could get a job in the US." His words said one thing, but the expression on his face told Michael a whole lot more, and the warm feeling in Michael's heart bumped up a notch. He'd seen Stephan with his family, and he knew what they meant to him. That he was willing to leave the continent to be with him told Michael everything he needed to know.

"Yes. I think you could get a job, but I don't want you to do that."

"Oh," Stephan said, turning back to look out the window. "At least you told me now."

It took Michael a few seconds before he realized what Stephan was getting at. "No. That's not what I meant. I thought I would see if I could get a job here."

"That's what you've been thinking about?" Stephan shifted on his seat. "You know you could have told me what you were thinking. I've been trying to figure out if I could go to the States with you." Stephan pouted slightly, and Michael wanted to kiss and suck that stuck-out lower lip.

"I should have talked to you. I guess I'm so used to being in charge that I just do it." Maybe that had been his problem with his past relationships. Michael reached over, quickly caressing that protruding lip with his thumb. "After our visit this weekend, it's obvious to me you're very close to your family, much closer to your family than I am to mine. Besides, I had a talk with your mother and that's what she told me to do. Now, since I have no intention of getting on your mother's bad side, I need to keep my promise."

Stephan looked at him in complete disbelief. "You had a talk with my mother? She doesn't really speak English." For a minute Stephan's eyes blazed. "You somehow managed to talk to my mother about what you wanted to do, but you never talked to me," Stephan said with an edge to his voice that Michael had never heard before.

Michael sighed to himself. This was not how he'd anticipated this discussion would go. "I know." Michael had no idea how to explain it. "I guess you had to be there." Michael reached over, taking Stephan's hand. "I love you, Stephan, and your mother helped me see that I needed to get off the fence and make a decision. That is, if you'll have me. I know I should have talked to you, and maybe if I had, I wouldn't have worried about it quite so much. I'm sorry."

Stephan's expression softened somewhat. "You'd really move here for me."

Michael nodded. "Yes. I know I really should have talked to you, and I thought about it, but especially after this weekend and meeting your family. It's funny, though neither of your parents spoke much English, I think I'd like to have them as my parents. I couldn't tell you why...." Michael steered the car onto the freeway. "Actually, I can. Your mom saw us kissing, and instead of freaking out like she could have, she talked to you, and her concern was your happiness. So I know I'm a little late, but yeah, I'd really move here."

Stephan flashed him a grin that outshone the sun. "Really? You aren't tugging my leg?" Stephan said, and Michael chuckled, relief flooding through him.

"No, I'm not pulling your leg. I really like it here. Unfortunately, I don't know if it'll work out, but I'm going to try."

"Then I'll help." Stephan told him, his expression half daring Michael to argue with him. "So what is the plan of attack?"

"I'm not really sure. I can speak with Greg tomorrow and see if there are any openings for a project manager, but I somehow doubt there are right now. Budgets are tight, and I think they brought me here in the first place because Greg didn't have the money in his budget to hire someone. It doesn't hurt to ask, though. Beyond that, I don't have any contacts outside of Shoe Box, so I'm not sure where to start looking."

"I can ask Kai," Stephan offered. "I know he's been impressed with the job you're doing, and he has contacts just about everywhere. Talking to him might have one more benefit—management makes decisions here together, so if Kai knows you are interested in staying, maybe he'll talk to the right people too." Excitement bloomed on Stephan's face for a few seconds before fading away. "None of this may help at all, and you may need to leave anyway."

Michael nodded. "I know. But we need to try. If we don't try, I'll go home in a few months, and if we do, the worst that can happen is that I still have to go home in a few months." Michael knew he was stating the obvious, and while he'd hoped it would make him feel better, it didn't.

"Can we talk about something else for a while?" Stephan asked, and Michael nodded and smiled, listening as Stephan pointed out the sights as they passed. They talked of nothing and everything, passing the time together. More than once, Michael felt his worries intruding on his thoughts, and he pushed them aside, determined to enjoy the last day of their vacation together.

Approaching Vianen, Michael exited the freeway, driving to Stephan's apartment. The one thing they hadn't talk about was what they were doing that evening, if anything. They'd spent the entire week together, and Michael couldn't blame Stephan if he wanted some time to himself, but almost as soon as they'd carried Stephan's bags inside, Stephan closed the door, and Michael found his arms filled with the man he loved. Kissing while standing in the living area quickly escalated to making out on the sofa, then to making love on the living room rug. Thankfully, Michael had some clean clothes he could wear to work the next day.

IN THE morning, Michael and Stephan dressed quietly, and drove to the office together. Saying good-bye in the car with a kiss, they walked into the office, giving each other a smile as they headed toward their departments. Michael booted up his computer and spent much of a quiet hour catching up on his e-mail and messages, answering what he could, filing others for a later reply.

"How was your holiday?" Greg asked, popping his head into the office.

"Fun and very relaxing," Michael answered, wondering if now was a good time to speak to him, before everyone else arrived. Figuring no time like the present, Michael got up and followed Greg to his office. "I'd like to ask you something."

Greg set his bag on the table before sitting in his chair, motioning for Michael to have a seat. "What can I do for you?"

Michael figured the direct approach was best. "I was wondering if you could use a good project manager."

"You?" Greg asked seriously, and Michael nodded once, waiting to see Greg's response. "I can't say this comes as a surprise, but I hadn't expected you to ask so early," Greg told him, as Michael looked him over intently, almost studying the other man, looking for any sign of hope. "I would like nothing more than to have you as a project manager on my staff. There are so many projects I'd like to do, and there's no one to run them, but right now there's no money in the budget." That was the answer Michael had expected, but it still hurt to actually hear it. Michael swallowed hard, nodding softly in understanding. He really couldn't have expected a different answer.

"Thank you, Greg. I understand," Michael said as he stood up, walking back toward the door. He needed to get out and be alone for a while to collect his thoughts. He knew he'd had no right to hope for a different answer and that he'd gotten the only answer that made sense. Michael opened the door, schooling his face to hide his emotions before walking back to his office, saying good morning to the others as he passed. He'd been foolish to allow any hope at all. As he reached his office, Michael quietly closed the door before going back to work. He had so much to do, he simply couldn't put it off, but he knew his emotions were written on his face as clear as day and right now he couldn't bear to have everyone who passed his office see them. Eventually, the work soothed him and his mind cleared.

Before lunch, Stephan knocked quietly, looking in questioningly, and Michael shook his head. Stephan entered the office, closing the door behind him. "I talked to Kai, and he told me pretty much the same thing Greg told you. But he did say that things can change and that if he heard of a proposal to add a project manager for IS, he'd support it. He also said that he'd keep his ear open for anything."

"I know it's a long shot," Michael said softly, "but I'd really like to work here." Stephan looked as forlorn as Michael felt. "We still have months, and a lot can change in that time."

"So what do we do?"

"We make the best of it." Michael stepped closer, touching Stephan's cheek lightly. Stephan closed his eyes, and Michael felt him lean into the touch. Then he straightened up, looked at Michael again with his big, beautiful brown eyes, and left the office without saying another word. Michael didn't know what to say, and he wanted to stop

Stephan and tell him it would be all right, if only to wipe the sad expression off his face.

Michael spent the rest of the day in his office. One of the office assistants brought him a sandwich from the cafeteria as Michael tried to catch up on everything he'd missed over the last week. That evening, he finally felt caught up, though exhausted. Getting up, he wandered to the marketing area and saw a single work light illuminating Stephan's dark hair. "Are you ready to go?" Michael asked, and Stephan got up, shutting off his light before following Michael out of the building.

Michael drove Stephan to his apartment, dropping him off before heading through Utrecht to his own. He'd hoped Stephan would come with him, but Michael knew he needed some time to think, and he figured Stephan did as well. At his apartment, Michael unloaded the car and started a load of laundry before making himself something to eat. He wished Stephan were there, and he wished he'd gotten better news, but there was nothing he could do about either. His heart kept looking for Stephan, expecting him to be just around every corner, and his mind told him he should distance himself so he didn't get hurt. Tired of thinking and stewing, he picked up his phone and called his mother. He hadn't talked to his family since before he'd left on holiday.

"Hi, Mom," Michael said when she answered. "I'm back from vacation safe and sound."

"Good. I'm so glad. Did you have a good time?"

"I did. We saw some amazing stuff." Michael went on to describe some of their travels. "I really called because I wanted to ask you something. I need your advice. I know we haven't been particularly close lately, with living in different parts of the country and now me in Europe, but I need your help."

She sniffled slightly on the other end. "Distance can be hard, but it doesn't mean I love you any less."

"I know, and I promise to call more often. When I get back to the States, I promise to come visit you and Dad."

"Your father and I were thinking that maybe we could come visit you for Christmas." He could almost see his mother's smile.

"I'd really like that." Michael hadn't really realized how far apart they'd grown until then. He was busy; they were busy. It was easy to not talk and drift apart.

"So what is it you want to ask me?" Michael's mother inquired after putting down the phone to blow her nose.

Michael told her about Stephan and how he felt. The timer went off on the oven, and Michael turned it off with his foot, leaving his food in to keep it hot before continuing his story, grateful that today he had a strong cell signal. "I'm not sure what to do."

"Do you love him?" she asked.

"So much it hurts, Mom."

"But is it enough?" she asked him.

"I don't understand," Michael told her, but she didn't say anything, and Michael checked that he hadn't lost the connection. "Mom, are you there?"

He heard breathing on the line for just a second. "Then let me ask this. If you have to leave him behind, is he worth the heartbreak and pain?" she asked softly. "If you leave, you'll be hurt, but is the time the two of you have together worth the hurt?"

Michael only had to think for a second. "Yes. He's worth it." Michael wondered if the answer could be that simple, but as he thought, he realized it was. Yes, Stephan was worth it, and it was that simple. "Thank you, Mom."

"You're welcome." They talked for a while as Michael got his dinner out of the oven and began to eat as he listened to her tell him all about everyone in the family and the people he'd grown up with, and Michael felt closer to her when he hung up than he had in a long time. Finishing his dinner, he thought of calling Stephan, and even picked up the phone twice, but stopped himself.

Michael rinsed the dishes before wandering into his bedroom and then into the bathroom, where he turned on the hot water for a bath. He never took baths by choice, but he needed to relax and he thought the warm water would help. Stripping off his clothes, Michael stepped into the bath before lowering himself into the tub, the warm water covering his skin. As he sighed softly from the heat, he heard his phone ringing in the other room. Getting out of the water, he wrapped a towel around his waist, reaching the phone just in time. "Michael, it's me," he heard Stephan say, with doubt and hurt in his voice. "I miss you."

"I miss you too," Michael replied as he dripped water all over the floor. "I was just in the bath when you called. Do you want to come over?"

"I hoped you would say that. I will be there in ten minutes," Stephan told him, and Michael smiled, some of the butterflies leaving his stomach. "Keep the bath water hot." The line disconnected, leaving Michael standing in his living room in only a towel, throbbing to beat the band.

The buzzer sounded eleven minutes later. Michael knew because he'd watched the clock change numbers between emptying the tub and running fresh hot water. Pressing the button to let Stephan in, Michael waited for the soft knock and then opened the door, practically pulling Stephan inside and into his arms.

Their kiss was bruisingly hard as Michael immediately began removing Stephan's clothes. By the time they reached the bathroom, a trail of clothes led from the front door to the bedroom. Michael knew the plan was for a bath, but Michael couldn't wait that long. As soon as he got Stephan onto the bed, he reached for a condom from the nightstand, and with Stephan urging him on the entire time, sank into his lover's greedy body.

The fast and furious lovemaking left them both huffing hard, and they lay on the bed, eyes closed, barely able to move. Michael eventually managed to get up and into the bathroom. Testing the bathwater, he ran some additional hot water before going into the bedroom. Beautiful didn't begin to describe how Stephan looked, his skin rich against the white sheets. Running his hand over Stephan's arm, he saw Stephan blink at him. "The bath is all set," Michael told him as he leaned over the bed, lightly touching Stephan's lips.

Together, they walked into the bathroom. Michael slipped into the tub, sitting back so Stephan could settle in front of him. It was a little cramped, but the warm water and Stephan's skin both felt wonderful. "Did you get a chance to think?" Michael asked as he fished the washcloth out of the water.

"All I thought about was you," Stephan admitted, chuckling lightly, and Michael added slightly more pressure to his washing so he wouldn't tickle.

"I thought about you, too, and I came to a conclusion," Michael said, and Stephan turned in the bath, their eyes meeting as he nodded. "You're worth it. If there's pain at the end, if I have to go, I won't regret anything, because you're worth it."

"You're worth it too," Stephan told him, their lips getting closer before coming together in a kiss.

# CHAPTER
## *Thirteen*

THE days and weeks slid by, each one going faster and faster, or at least that was how it felt to Michael. His projects went very well, and the Shoe Finder system went in for its initial pilot with minimal issues, which made Michael, along with Mark, Greg, and the rest of the European management team, happy. Michael even got a few leads on other jobs, but they didn't seem to pan out. "Congratulations, Michael," Greg called, as they met outside the office and walked inside together. "The system really works and the stores love it."

"Thanks," Michael responded, as they walked through the automatic doors and up to their offices. "And now that we have the special software for Italy working, we should be able to finish on time." He knew he should be happy beyond belief, and he would have been if he were the same person who'd originally come here five months earlier, but he wasn't. The reason he'd come here in the first place was nearly complete, and he was supposed to go home in a few weeks. But everything had truly changed for him. However, he'd come to accept that he was going to have to leave and that he'd have to say good-bye to Stephan.

Last night, when they were in Stephan's apartment, curled together in the dark, Stephan had asked him if he regretted anything.

"Are you asking if I regret meeting you? Because the answer is no. I will never regret meeting you. Once I go home it will be hard for me, very hard, but the last months have been the best of my life." Michael held Stephan close, his eyes filling with tears, but he wouldn't let himself cry. Michael had known he would feel this way, and he'd willingly signed up for it. "Do you regret anything?" Michael had asked, trying to keep his voice steady.

"No, I do not." Stephan had curled close to him, and they'd continued holding one another long into the night. Michael hadn't slept much the past few nights, and last night was no exception.

Michael covered a yawn with his hand as he set his computer bag on the desk before pulling out his laptop. Booting it up, Michael got to work, doing what he did whenever his mind wasn't engaged in something else—thinking of Stephan. As he checked his messages, he noticed an invitation from Greg for their regular weekly one-on-one session. Noticing that it was in an hour, Michael finished looking through his e-mail before preparing for the meeting. Printing copies of the updated plans and timelines, Michael knocked on Greg's open door before stepping inside. Closing the door, Michael took a seat.

"According to the schedule, it looks like the project is going to be completed on time. No thanks to your ex-boss," Greg said, leaning toward Michael. "I thought you should know that Mark contacted me last week about Curtis, and I shared the e-mail that you received with him. Mark seemed very interested, and it appears he had some of his own suspicions. He used the information from you to help build his case, and last night was Curtis's last day with the company."

Michael wanted to jump up and do a happy dance, but he settled for a smile and a nod. Then they got down to the remaining details of Michael's project.

THAT evening, Michael met Stephan at his apartment, knocking quietly before waiting for Stephan to open the door. After knocking a second time, he heard footsteps on the stairs. The door opened and Stephan gasped.

"I brought you tulips," Michael said, stating the obvious as he handed Stephan the huge bouquet with a gigantic grin.

Stephan took them, smiling as he carried the flowers up the stairs. "No one's ever brought me flowers before."

"Then it's about time," Michael quipped as they reached the top, walking into Stephan's living room.

"Is there a special occasion I forgot?" Stephan asked as he walked into the kitchen, rummaging in the cupboards for a vase. "Where did you find tulips?"

"At the flower shop in Vianen. I called to make sure they could get them. But to answer your first question, the special occasion is that you're looking at the new project manager for Shoe Box Europe."

Stephan stilled for a few seconds before standing up and turning around. The flowers dropped onto the counter, and Michael heard a squeal before Stephan barreled into him, hugging and kissing him within an inch of his life. "You can really stay?"

"Yes, I can really stay," Michael said with a laugh as they tumbled together onto the sofa, with Stephan squirming on top of him as they continued kissing.

"When did you find out?"

"I had my regular meeting with Greg this morning. He told me that Curtis has been let go, and then we talked over the details of the upcoming project tasks. We must have talked for an hour, and at the end of the meeting, he slid a piece of paper across his desk. It was the job offer. He made me wait all the way through the meeting, saying nothing about it until the end."

Stephan squirmed away, glaring down at him.

"What?" Michael asked, and Stephan smacked him on the shoulder.

"You made me wait until now." Stephan managed to suppress his smile for about two seconds.

"I'm sorry. I wanted to surprise you properly, and I kept feeling like this was too good to be true," Michael said before pulling Stephan back onto the sofa. "There's only one thing."

"What?" Stephan asked, meeting Michael's eyes.

"I need to find a place to live." Michael smiled, and Stephan grinned right back before kisses stopped the rest of the conversation.

# Epilogue

"STEPHAN," Michael called as he opened the outside door before climbing the stairs to what had been Stephan's apartment, now their apartment. Yes, it was small, but Michael thought of it as their cozy love nest. When he got no answer, Michael took off his coat before setting his bag in its place. With an apartment this small, Michael had learned very quickly that everything had its place and it had to go there. Hanging up his coat, he walked into the kitchen to make dinner.

A lot of things had changed for Michael in the past few months. Some of his things had been shipped over, and Stephan had graciously made room for them. He hadn't shipped much—just enough so that the apartment felt as though it belonged to both of them. Most of the rest of his things he'd either sold or put in storage with his parents. He'd also learned how to cook. Well, a few things. Opening the refrigerator, Michael had begun pulling out the ingredients for dinner when he heard the door open downstairs and multiple sets of feet tromping up the stairs. Stephan stepped into the living area first, followed by Michael's mom and dad.

"That was amazing," Michael's mother, Sue, commented as she slipped out of her coat. "It looked like the whole of Amsterdam was decked out for the holidays."

"I take it you had a good time," Michael said as he hugged first his mother and then his dad.

"So you're done working?" his dad, Clark, asked as he sat down in the living room.

"Yes. We're both off for the next week right through Christmas. The weather looks nice for the next few days, so is anyone up for a small trip?" Michael looked at the faces around the room, pausing for dramatic effect. "I thought we could drive to Cologne to the Christmas market and spend the night." Michael saw his mother's eyes light up, and his dad rolled his eyes. "The market is right near the cathedral, Dad. You can spend as much time there as you like." Now his dad smiled. "Something for everyone," Michael added with a grin, turning to Stephan before pulling him close. "I already got hotel reservations," Michael said as he nibbled Stephan's ear. "Our room has something special," Michael added, just for Stephan.

"It's very sweet of your mother to have us for Christmas. I'm dying to meet her," Sue told Stephan as she muscled them both out of the kitchen so she could take over making dinner.

"Of course. She's very excited too," Stephan answered.

"Mom, you remember that Stephan's parents don't speak much English," Michael cautioned.

"We speak the same language. We're both mothers," she countered, closing the door on that conversation.

Michael and Stephan let her make dinner, joining his dad in the living room and talking about their day. His parents had gotten in two days earlier, resting the first day and spending today with Stephan in Amsterdam. Michael had wanted to join them, but he'd had things he had to get done before his holiday vacation.

Sue brought in plates, and they ate in the living area since the table was only big enough for two. Afterward, Stephan took the plates in the kitchen, leaving them alone, or as alone as anyone could get in the small apartment. "I'm glad you're happy," his mother told him as Michael watched Stephan move in the kitchen.

"I am, Mom, I really am," Michael answered her softly, not looking away from the kitchen. "I've known him for less than a year, and I couldn't imagine my life without him."

"It's a shame you're so far away, but it's good to see you in love," she said, patting his knee before getting up. "We should get back to our hotel. I'm tired, and we have a big day tomorrow."

Michael handed his father the keys to his car and gave him directions to the hotel. After getting their coats and sharing more hugs, they left, leaving Stephan and Michael alone. It was like someone flicked a switch and they were in each other's arms, hugging, holding, and kissing on their way to the bedroom. "I missed seeing you today," Michael whispered between kisses, working Stephan's clothes off. "I kept looking for you even though I knew you weren't there." Stephan's pants hit the floor, his belt clinking. As Stephan stepped out of his jeans, Michael got his shirt off and managed somehow to get out of his pants before tackling a very naked and sexy Stephan onto the bed.

"*Ik hou van je,*" Michael sighed into Stephan's kiss, and he could feel Stephan's love coming back to him without words.

"*Ik hou van je,*" Stephan repeated against his lips as Michael's hands cupped the curve of Stephan's butt. Then words failed; they were not needed, anyway. Michael had come to Europe on business, not expecting he'd find the unequivocal love of his life.

"Sometimes I still cannot believe you are here," Stephan told him, his eyes blazing.

"Well, I am, and I'm never going to leave you," Michael answered, pulling Stephan into another kiss. He'd found his very own Dutch treat, and by God he wasn't about to let him go.

ANDREW GREY grew up in western Michigan with a father who loved to tell stories and a mother who loved to read them. Since then he has lived throughout the country and traveled throughout the world. He has a master's degree from the University of Wisconsin-Milwaukee and works in information systems for a large corporation. Andrew's hobbies include collecting antiques, gardening, and leaving his dirty dishes anywhere but in the sink (particularly when writing). He considers himself blessed with an accepting family, fantastic friends, and the world's most supportive and loving partner. Andrew currently lives in beautiful historic Carlisle, Pennsylvania.

Visit Andrew's web site at http://www.andrewgreybooks.com and blog at http://andrewgreybooks.livejournal.com/. E-mail him at andrewgrey@comcast.net.

Contemporary Romance by ANDREW GREY

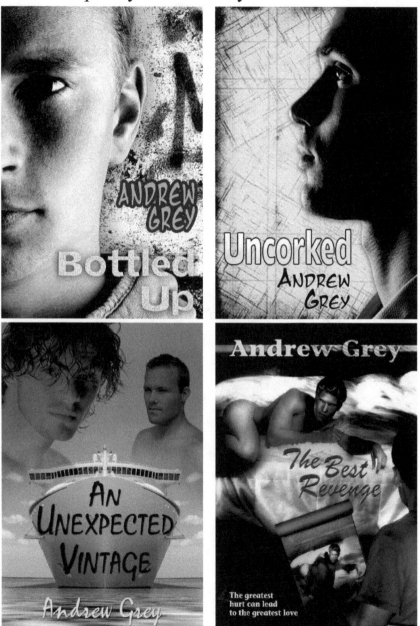

http://www.dreamspinnerpress.com

Contemporary Romance by ANDREW GREY

http://www.dreamspinnerpress.com

# Also by ANDREW GREY

http://www.dreamspinnerpress.com

Contemporary Romance by ANDREW GREY

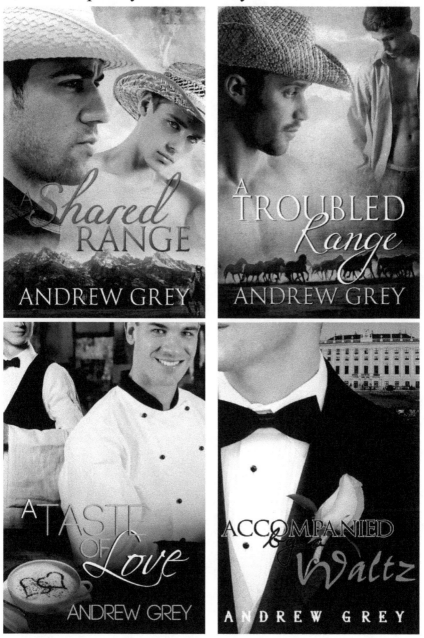

Contemporary Fantasy by ANDREW GREY

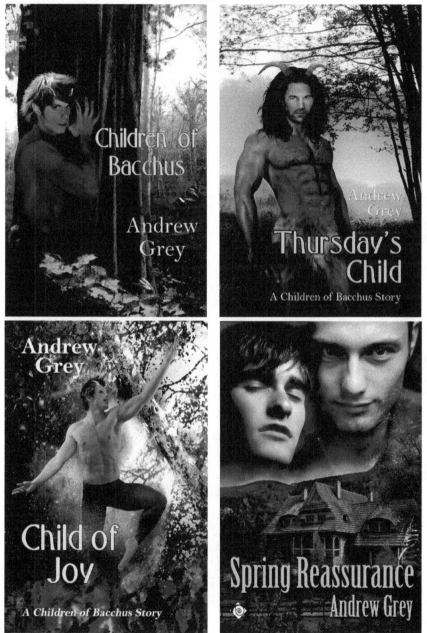

http://www.dreamspinnerpress.com

CPSIA information can be obtained
at www.ICGtesting.com
Printed in the USA
LVHW04s2328150618
580542LV00010B/43/P

9 781613 720578